Anonymous

A Cry from the Land of Calvin and Voltaire

a sequal

Anonymous

A Cry from the Land of Calvin and Voltaire
a sequal

ISBN/EAN: 9783337339913

Printed in Europe, USA, Canada, Australia, Japan

Cover: Foto ©Andreas Hilbeck / pixelio.de

More available books at **www.hansebooks.com**

A CRY FROM THE LAND

OF

CALVIN AND VOLTAIRE:

A SEQUEL TO " THE WHITE FIELDS OF FRANCE."

Records of the McAll Mission.

WITH INTRODUCTION BY THE

REV. HORATIUS BONAR, D.D.

"There stood a man of [France], and prayed him, saying, Come over into [France], and help us."—ACTS xvi. 9.

WITH EIGHT ILLUSTRATIONS.

London:

HODDER AND STOUGHTON,

27, PATERNOSTER ROW.

MDCCCLXXXVII.

EDINBURGH: MACNIVEN AND WALLACE;
PARIS: OFFICES OF THE MISSION, 28, VILLA MOLITOR, AUTEUIL.

CONTENTS.

PROFESSOR ROSSEEUW ST. HILAIRE,

Member of the Institute of France.

December, 1881.

" Never before has there been such liberty in France to spread the Gospel. There is now freedom for meetings of all kinds, for those in which religion is defended as well as for those in which it is assailed ; and those you have founded have been surrounded by protection and respect under all the political changes. Protestantism—rather, let us say, the religion of Christ—is now, so to speak, in the air one breathes in France. A breath of revival has passed over our torpid population, and the Gospel is everywhere welcomed. . . . In the departments as well as in the capital the holy contagion spreads from day to day."

December, 1882.

" It was the Lord Himself who put it into your heart to attempt such a work alone and without human aid—if, indeed, we are alone when God is with us ! Throwing yourself, with your beloved wife, into an enterprise the spread and issues of which you could little foresee, a voluntary exile, far from your country, in Belleville, that notorious suburb, the volcano, far from extinct, in which all the animosities and passions of the Commune were still brooding, . . . you did not fear to plant the Gospel standard ; and your daring, inspired from on high, was the sure pledge of your success. God has blessed your enterprise beyond all you could have hoped for. In addressing yourself to the poor, the ignorant, the outcasts of this world, like our Master, you have gained the ear of all. . . . The resident pastors have enrolled themselves with you in this noble undertaking ; and, after laying siege to Paris, you have sought to conquer France. Already a considerable number of the great towns possess your mission stations, which are everywhere gladly welcomed ; and if one, at least, has not been opened in each department, it is only the funds and the workers that have been lacking, not the desire and appeal of the inhabitants, anxious to partake, in their turn, the blessings of the Gospel."

INTRODUCTION.

BY THE REV. HORATIUS BONAR, D.D.

I T is just seventy years ago since Robert Haldane, of Edinburgh, after labouring, along with his brother James, as an evangelist in Scotland, turned his steps to the Continent of Europe. His expansive energies could not be confined within the limits of this northern fragment of Great Britain. His earnest eye went over other lands, and he could not rest till he had attempted something for the evangelising of the cities of France. He had not sold his splendid Scottish estate in vain.

He set out alone. He went chiefly as an explorer of an unknown region, and he passed the Channel when the last echoes of the great Napoleonic battles had just died away. In 1816 he proceeded to Paris to inquire into the religious state of the people, and the possibilities of access for the Gospel into the midst of their pleasure-loving millions. The sounds of war had ceased. Would not this be a singularly favourable opportunity for proclaiming the Gospel of peace ?

But he found no entrance for the messengers of the Cross. Every gate was barred. The god of this world held the ramparts and guarded the gates. The strong man armed was on the watch.

So he went his way, thinking Paris quite hopeless,

I

and its strongholds impregnable, as indeed they truly seemed to be. He turned his steps to Geneva, and in Switzerland he found, if not quite a welcome, at least an open door. Yet it was hard to say whether Parisian Popery or Genevan Rationalism were the more impenetrable in their resistance to the light of Christ. He could not say of the Swiss cities, " A great door and effectual is opened to me ; " but he could rejoice in being made the instrument of raising up such witnesses as Malan and Merle d'Aubigné, with others of like outstanding eminence, who shone in after-days as lights not only in Geneva, but in Europe. He would have stayed in Paris to work there ; " but the Spirit suffered him not." The work for Paris was not to be done by him, nor in his day. Yet it was to be done as quietly, by as simple instruments, through the faith of one man. The door that he found shut was to be thrown open in the next generation, and the message for which he could find no entrance was to penetrate each lane of the city, and, going beyond its walls and suburbs, was to make its way into the cities and villages of the kingdom, far and near.

Robert Haldane would certainly be amazed were he to return and behold what God has done for that France of which he utterly despaired.

Every day brings us news from different quarters of Europe of light springing out of darkness. It is not France merely from which these rays are coming forth. All over Europe we detect the same blessed streaks, not only in its great cities, but in many of its provincial towns and humble villages. As we wander over the Continent, or read the letters of Christian travellers, we are amazed to find the extent to which the Gospel has been diffused, not by Societies merely or large organisations, but by solitary Christians, who carried Christ with them wherever they went, and who left behind them the blessed footprints of Christian devotedness. Continental darkness is great ; but there are streaks of light.

These scattered sparks of unexpected Gospel radiance, feeble, but very bright, remind one of the fire-flies that sparkle in the darkness of an Italian landscape from its hedges as you traverse its highways and byways. The evangelistic intelligence from the Continent becomes daily more interesting. Popery is not now the dense, dark, impenetrable cloud that it was in the last generation ; and even infidelity, which is fast becoming a power more terrible than Popery, is opening its doors to the messengers of the Cross.

The condition of Europe is becoming more critical and chaotic. The fermentation going on, religious, political, ecclesiastical, threatens the dissolution of all order and peace. But in the midst of all this the Gospel is working its way everywhere, the elect of God are being gathered in, and the purpose of God regarding the ten kingdoms of Daniel's fourth empire is being rapidly fulfilled. We may expect a large inbringing, not from France only, not from the Continent only, but from all regions of the globe.

The forces of evil are no longer dormant. The god of this world is mustering his armies. The inertness which in many places marked the past generation has given way. The ice is broken up; and the issues of a strange and stormy futurity are crowding down upon us. We do not need to attempt being prophets in order to foretell the confusion which is at hand.

Yet the world's extremity is God's opportunity. The amount of evil is no cause of despair. Our messengers do not go forth in despondency to discharge a thankless errand. They may sow in tears, but they shall reap in joy; they may often be weary and sorrowful, but they shall return from the harvest-field bringing their sheaves with them.

The world is not at rest. Far off and near we see the signs of disquietude, the elements of confusion— truth and error at war with each other; righteousness and unrighteousness brought face to face; good and evil mixed up together, and contending for the mastery; universal fermentation both spiritually and politically; the nations shaking their swords at each other, and only restrained from fierce warfare by some unseen power, some mysterious influence superior to their own power and wisdom; men's passions in full play, breaking out in all directions, producing distrust and disgrace and sad foreboding of what is coming on the earth, "men's hearts failing them for fear, and for looking after the things that are coming on the earth," "the sea and its waves roaring."

Is the Christian to sit down and take no notice of these prognostications? Is he to say, "We cannot help these things; they must just go on as they have been doing; the storms will exhaust themselves by-and-by, and peace will come in the course of nature. Meanwhile let us not disturb ourselves with what we cannot help, but just go on in our ordinary ways, hoping for the best, shutting our eyes against the threatening storms, and our ears against the prophets of evil"?

Whatever be the forebodings of evil, the Christian man has a word to speak and a work to do. It may look very hopeless, and to be confronted with such a mass of evil as Europe now presents *is* enough to dismay us. But "Go forward" is the watchword given to us, as it was to Israel of old. The sea, with its dark depths, was before them; Pharaoh, with his chariots and horsemen, was behind them ; and the towering ridge of mountains was at their right. All was hopeless. But the word came, "Go forward;" and they went. The sea divided, the dry land appeared, and every enemy was swept away. So does the command come to the Christian in our day of ungodliness and infidelity, "Go forward." There is the work, and God commands! It is thus in faith that Mr. McAll and his brave comrades are acting. It is only faith that enables them to hold on in the face of foes who outnumber them by tens of thousands. "It is the Christian's cowardice that spoils his fortune," writes one when speaking of a man of faith. Let no such cowardice be ours. Cowardice belongs to unbelief, not to faith ; the believing man is by his very nature brave.

It is only from such narratives as those of the McAll Mission and kindred institutions that we learn the inner religious life of France, whether deep or shallow, whether great or small. Its outer life we may gather from its churches and cathedrals, or even from its street literature and daily journals. But that outer life is of little interest to the Church of God, save as exhibiting the vast field of evil which the Christian worker has to cultivate.

Church history, as it has usually been written, has been more a history of error than of truth, of strife and controversy rather than of "peace on earth and good-will to men." It has been the annals of human

ambition, and pride, and selfishness, mingled with
religious names and doctrines, in which the name of
Christ may appear, but in which the spirit and life of
Christ find no place. Hence those whom ecclesiastical
history has honoured with the name of "fathers" are
not the true representatives of the living Church, but
frequently its persecutors ; not the witnesses for the
truth of God, but the propagators of error ; not
specimens of " the woman who fled into the wilderness
from the face of the serpent," but of the serpent which
sought to slay her and her seed.

So throughout Europe, and especially through France,
it is not to the seats of learning nor the schools of
theology, not to the Academy nor the Sorbonne, not
to the stately Abbey, with its noble organ, and well-
equipped choir, and priestly vestments, that we go to
discover the spiritual life of the community. That
which the eye of God holds precious is something
apart from all these, something hidden from the common
view, something which only the discriminating eye of
faith can recognise as Divine. Externalism bulks
mightily in the general eye ; grandeur and beauty,
whether in sound or sight, captivate the natural man.
The vesture of religion is mistaken for religion itself,
so that one passing from city to city and viewing
cathedral after cathedral throughout Europe would
say, " What an amount of religion is here ! what an
assemblage of religious nations ! These piles of carved
stones, these ornamented arches, these splendid gate-
ways, these gorgeous altars, that marvellous music,
these solemn choirs,—what a vast amount of piety do
they represent ! "

But is there no hollowness here ? And is not all

this show intended to make up for the unreality and to hide the hollowness? The magnificence of the Milan cathedral, instead of being the representative of spiritual life, may be a mere religious petrefaction, a conglomeration of religious ideas carved in stone to commemorate the spirit which had gone out of those who thus, perhaps with aching hearts and weary hands, endeavoured to perpetuate a faith which in themselves was nothing but a name.

No, we must go to humbler edifices in order to get hold of the religious life of a land. It is not in sacerdotal pomps that life is embalmed, nor in architectural splendour that the Spirit of God is enshrined.

We go to Notre Dame on some festal day. We admire its grandeur. Interior and exterior are perfect. We gaze on the crowds listening and kneeling. We hear the roll of the organ and the melody of the choir. Do we come away saying, "What an amount of religion is here! How acceptable to God"? Perhaps we do; but perhaps others have their misgivings. Is it all real? Is not all this amount of show and sound fitted to produce unreality? Must we not go elsewhere to find the true and the spiritual?

We turn into one of the *salles* whose bright light meets our eye. It only holds three or four hundred. It is an old wineshop turned into a hall. It is clean, cheery, and well-lighted. The speaker is in earnest. He is uttering the words of everlasting life. There is no hollowness here. The eager eyes of the audience show that his words are finding their way into the hearts of the hearers. Converse with one of them. He will tell you of the wondrous change which words like these have wrought in him. The love of God has come into his soul and filled it. He has found his way to the true Cross, and there he rests. Peace in believing is his portion now. He has got a religion which makes him glad. He now knows what it is to pray and praise. He has found in the Bible a wondrous Book, on which he meditates without ceasing. His outward life is changed. His family life is transformed. He is a different husband and father and neighbour from what he used to be.

Thus in these Mission *salles* we discover seeds, hidden ones, and learn the secret of a nation's true life.

Three centuries ago it was the earthquake that shook Europe. Now it is the still small voice. Everywhere through the world that voice is now heard ; and it is telling in wondrous ways and by strange, often feeble instruments. It is the power of God unto salvation, and it is going forth amid the confusion of earth for the ingathering of God's elect. It will prove itself mightier than the mighty sounds of the world. It is irresistible. Not eloquence, nor learning, nor science, but the simplicity of the one Gospel,—it is this that is to do the great work. " Not the wisdom of this world" was the Apostle's motto when he went to Corinth. " Not the wisdom of this world" is our motto in these days of unbelief, and worldliness, and vanity.

" Nil desperandum" is our motto. We write it on our banners, and go forth against the multitudinous hosts of evil. " Thanks be unto God, who always causeth us to triumph in Christ." Thus it is that "we are more than conquerors through Him that loved us."

HORATIUS BONAR.

I.

THE CRY OF FRANCE ADDRESSED TO BRITISH CHRISTIANS.

BY THE REV. R. W. McALL.

"There stood a man of [France], and prayed him, saying, Come over into [France], and help us."—Acts xvi. 9.

The Evening Visit of the " Man of Macedonia" on the Outer Boulevards of Paris.

" SIR, are you not a Christian minister? If so, I have something of importance to say to you. You are, at this moment, in the very midst of a district inhabited by thousands and tens of thousands of us, working men. To a man we have done with an imposed religion, a religion of superstition and oppression. But if any one would come to teach us religion of another kind—a religion of freedom and earnestness— many of us are ready to listen."

Such were the words addressed to me on the evening of August 18th, 1871, as I stood with my wife at the point where the Rue de Belleville pours its living tide into the great highway of the outer boulevards of North Paris.* The entire surroundings, the half-dilapidated

---

* This scene is represented in the frontispiece, from the gifted pencil of M. Eugène Burnand, a young artist rapidly rising into

buildings, the thronged wine-vaults, the shop windows
displaying revolutionary newspapers and rude caricature
prints, the motley and often turbulent procession of
passers to and fro, may be considered by the rare
tourist hurrying past *en route* for Père Lachaise or the
Butte Chaumont as the ideal of all that is uninteresting
and repulsive. But for us the spot is memorable, even
sacred. Never, since that decisive evening, can we
tread it without profound emotion. Thenceforward the
whole current of our life was changed, and the foundation was laid of a movement the full issues of which
eternity alone can disclose.

Here is the history. I was an English pastor ; and
to none, I am convinced, could the pastoral relation and
work be dearer than they were to me. My wife and I
had crossed the Channel for the first time, on occasion
of our brief summer holiday. The last of the four days
allotted to Paris had come. But we were unwilling to
leave the city until we should have borne some testimony of our heart's yearning over those who had so
recently known the horrors of bloodshed and famine.
So we resolved to spend our last night in offering tracts
and Scripture portions in the ill-fated quarter, to which,
however, the one or two friends we then had in Paris
declined to accompany us. We stood there alone, or
rather One "like unto the Son of God" was, surely,
close beside us !

There was something remarkable, even providential,
respecting those tracts, which formed our effectual
introduction to the people. Before leaving England,
we had experienced difficulty in procuring them.

celebrity, and a devout Christian and zealous helper in the mission-
work. Others of the illustrations are also from his pencil.

Arrived in London, and the hour of the tidal train already near, we found ourselves without them. Only by a sharp run to St. Paul's Churchyard, to the depository of that great Society which has since rendered invaluable help to our work in supplying hundreds of thousands of these publications, did I procure the precious little parcel, an essential link in this unseen chain.

So there, under the windows of the great wineshop forming the angle of the Rue de Belleville and the Boulevard, my wife and I took our stand. The " blouses " were all around us. As yet few evidences of Christian interest had reached these remote and dreaded " citizens." What had been done was chiefly in supplies of food, etc., sent from England. Miss de Broen had, indeed, commenced shortly before her courageous and now extensive and much-blessed work in the district, but we were unaware of its existence, until we afterwards received letters of welcome from herself, when our intention became known to her. No sooner was a friendly purpose on our part recognised than large and eager groups gathered round us, desiring the tracts ; and we soon heard the exclamation (prompted, no doubt, by remembrance of the ambulances and the food-stores), " Bons Anglais ! "

The decisive moment had come, though we knew it not. The " man of Macedonia " awaited us. My wife having offered a tract to the waiter of the large corner wineshop, he begged her to enter, " for," said he, " each customer wished to possess one." Just as she emerged from the door, a working man, French, but, marvellous to say, speaking excellent English, stepped forward, and, in the name of the bystanders, addressed to me the identical words with which this volume commences. I never saw him afterwards, so far as I know; but his earnest bearing, each word, his very countenance, were engraved indelibly in my memory.

The immediate impression was powerful, but only prayerful reflection could make us alive to the sovereign mandate couched in those few sentences. Scarcely could Paul's "vision in the night" surpass the directness of this appeal: "Come over into France, and help us."

How wonderful! We might have walked the same streets and stood with our tracts at the same corner a thousand times, and not encountered the unique man. Why were our steps guided thither precisely at the moment of his passing? Ever since we have felt, beyond any previous realisation, that we are simply instruments in the Lord's hand, most unworthy to be so employed, but appointed to accomplish the Lord's purpose (for we had none of our own) on behalf of the disinherited and unsought of the sister nation.

The Sequel of our Evening Walk on the Outer Boulevards.

"Wife, I have found out a new religion, such a religion as I had no idea existed; it is so good, so beautiful. You must come also and learn all about it." These, literally translated, are the words of a business *employé*, a man in the prime of life, on his return home one night, ten or twelve years ago, from one of our Paris mission-rooms, which the gaslights and a kind word of invitation had induced him to enter. He had gone in hesitatingly, ignorant of the nature of the meeting. Everything had come to him as a surprising and gladdening discovery; the announcement

of free salvation through a dying Saviour's merits met
the before unsatisfied craving of his spirit. From that
time the husband and wife regularly attended, and their
two children were placed in our Sabbath-school at the
same station. Never shall I forget the new-found joy
imprinted on the man's features when, a few days afterwards, he grasped my hand and spoke forth his gratitude.
Could I fail to recognise in that precious soul, in that
family "brought out of darkness into marvellous light,"
a rich reward for having left people and country in
order to seek out these neglected but waiting ones?
Within about a year from that time, after severe and
protracted sufferings, borne with resignation, my humble
friend died in peaceful reliance on the Saviour to whom
we had been privileged to guide him. During his
painful illness he used to say that he had only one
wish—to be allowed, if it were God's will, to visit once
more "the dear meetings" ("les chères réunions").
When no longer able to speak, he raised his dying
hand heavenward.

Eleven years ago, one of our visitors entered the
small lodging of a workman who, with his family, had
commenced attendance at the meetings. She found
the place wretched and almost without furniture, the
husband having been addicted to intemperance. But
the wife stated that already, "since hearing of the
new religion," he had broken from his ruinous habit.
Shortly afterwards, on paying a second visit, our friend
found everything changed. Pointing to a new wardrobe, the wife asked, "Madam, what do you suppose
we call that? My husband and I call it Mr. McAll's
wardrobe ["l'armoire de M. McAll"], for we could
never have bought it had it not been for his meetings."

Such are the blessings even for " the life that now is " which the Gospel ever bears along with it.

Here, then, were some of those waiting ones, represented by our workman-pleader as " ready to listen if any one would come to teach a religion of freedom and earnestness." And, thank God, a multitude of others, of all ages and classes, have borne their diversified testimonies, both in Paris and throughout France, to the truth of those prophetic words.

It was, as I have said, on August 18th, 1871, that the Macedonian cry was addressed to us. After deep stirrings of spirit, and consultation with the late excellent Dr. Georges Fisch, of Paris, and other friends, we resolved to make the bold attempt in the name of our Divine Master. We chose for our residence a humble lodging in the very midst of the workmen's habitations. The very day we had hired our rooms a friend gave us the pleasing intelligence that it was a most dangerous quarter, and that nothing was more probable than our being assassinated in the streets! On the contrary, during seven years' residence in Belleville, we and our fellow-workers came and returned at all hours, and were invariably treated with the utmost respect. There was no novelty in the character of our meetings, except for these poor neglected ones, unused to religious services of every kind before. We had hymns, reading the Bible, short, pointed Gospel addresses (usually two, at least, in an hour's meeting), prayers, with the added feature of free lending libraries, children's religious gatherings, etc. Adopting an undenominational basis, we sought and speedily obtained the co-operation of French evangelical pastors and of the members of their Churches. And the same simplicity of organisation and procedure characterises the entire work to this day. Aiming primarily to attract the working classes, it has, naturally, along with its extension to diversified districts, and especially in the centre of Paris, come to embrace a wider social range. The majority of our stations are attended by the poorest of the poor, and these we, first of all, seek. But others of the mission-halls have for their congregations the well-to-do and educated classes, who, we rejoice to say, vie, in many cases, with their humbler neighbours in eager and serious attention.

On the afternoon of January 17th, 1872, Mrs. McAll and I walked the crowded Rue de Belleville, distributing small papers of invitation, of which the following is a reduced facsimile :—

AUX OUVRIERS !

RUE JULIEN-LACROIX, 103, BELLEVILLE.

DIMANCHE PROCHAIN, A 8 HEURES DU SOIR, UN AMI ANGLAIS DESIRE VOUS PARLER DE

L'AMOUR DE JESUS-CHRIST.

VOUS SEREZ TOUS LES BIENVENUS.

Une Bibliothèque gratuite sera ouverte de sept heures et demie à huit heures.

The same evening, I conducted my first French meeting in the little mission-hall (a shop) we had hired.

When the furnishing of this humble place was under consideration, our kind friend the Rev. T. Baron Hart offered to lend us chairs from his chapel. " How many will be needed ? " " Twenty or, at most, twenty-four will be amply sufficient," was the answer returned by sage counsellors. Twenty-eight of the neighbours came in. One or two young Englishmen helped us. Before the second evening (Sunday) we increased our chairs fourfold, and all were filled, for over one hundred persons thronged the room. Already we began to feel, with unspeakable joy, that the work, begun with trembling, but in faith, had taken root. I shall not here repeat our subsequent history. Suffice it to remark that if to-day we were again brought face to face with that Belleville workman, we could point him, as the direct fruit of his appeal, to nearly one hundred stations of our own Mission, besides not a few others more or less connected in origin with the impulse then received. We would say to him, " Behold, how great a matter a little fire has kindled ! Behold the issues of your earnest words addressed to two foreigners on the highway ! " And we should have to bid him look even beyond the boundaries of France proper,—to Corsica, to the African colonies, to Switzerland, to the French-speaking people of America.

Take a recent scene. From the wineshop door at the angle of the rude outer boulevard, let us pass into the magnificent Salle des Fêtes of the Trocadéro Palace. The date is May 13th, 1886. From the great platform, I look on the assembled thousands of the French Protestant Sunday scholars of Paris. One and another pastor asks, "Where are your mission-school children, Mr. McAll ? " I point to the vast amphitheatre of galleries outstretched before us, crowded to the ceiling, and reply, "They fill those galleries." As I spoke, I felt myself carried back in thought to our very first small gathering of poor children, February 1st, 1872, in which my wife and I were literally the only workers. The "little one" had, indeed, "become a thousand," and more than that. And these were only our elder scholars; the younger ones could not be brought from so great distances. Surveying that multitude, at once orderly and joyous, under the admirable leadership of the Rev. C. E. Greig and his lieutenant, M. Arthur de Rougemont, we recognised an oasis newly reclaimed from the moral waste, as nearly all belonged to families in which, apart from the mission effort, no Gospel teachings whatever existed. From every bright young countenance, and from the ringing chorus of their voices swelling the hymns, the old appeal of the boulevard returned upon us, with resistless urgency. It was as the voice of tens of thousands of unsought French children, not less accessible to Christian influence than these, repeating the cry, "Come over and help us." A purified and regenerated France in a new generation seemed to arise, prophetically, before us. If from the quiet resolve formed by two strangers, fifteen years ago, to give their lives to this work, so much, under God, has resulted, what might not be looked for could the Christians of more favoured lands be induced to send forth a host of labourers and to sustain the large band of faithful native workers who would not be far to seek, resolved to bear Heaven's regenerating message to every French home and heart?

Enough. My aim is not to magnify what God has

2

enabled us to accomplish. In view of the widespread spiritual destitution around us, it is only as a drop in the ocean. And, alas! how much of human imperfection has marked and hindered our efforts! But the case presents itself thus: What were we—we say it unfeignedly and most humbly—that we should be selected as the Holy Spirit's instruments in leading the van in this sacred campaign? Certainly we had no qualifications for its successful pursuit beyond those possessed by multitudes of our fellow-believers. Is it not clear as day that, in thus taking our life and our steps into His own hand, and leading us, by a way we knew not, to this issue, OUR LORD LOUDLY PROCLAIMS WHAT HE IS WAITING TO DO FOR FRANCE BY THE INSTRUMENTALITY OF OTHERS OF HIS CHILDREN?

Nationality and Evangelisation.

I was present, not long ago, at a well-attended Sunday night prayer-meeting in an English seaport immediately opposite the French coast. I was moved to say, " On a clear day, you can *distinctly see*, across the ocean, the spot where there is a town of between 40,000 and 50,000 inhabitants, the vast majority of whom have literally never heard the Gospel; they have no idea what it is. If such a place existed, involved in similar spiritual destitution, little more than twenty miles away, *on your own side the Channel*, would you not recognise a paramount call to arise and seek, by toil and self-sacrifice, to make its people, 'perishing for lack of knowledge,' sharers of the heavenly treasure you possess? That town," I added, " DOES exist; those needs press to the utmost; only the waves roll between. Commerce braves that expanse of waters. Even the instinct of pleasure-seeking treats it as of small account. Shall love to souls be bounded and held in by it? Do not those cliffs on the horizon proclaim unfaithfulness on your part? Is not the Macedonian cry borne to you on every evening breeze, ' Come over and help us ' ? "

So far as I could discover, not an individual in the meeting even knew of the existence of our Branch Mission in that French town, not one had ever made the smallest attempt to convey a ray of heavenly light across the waters !

I advance the bold assertion—but who shall dispute it ?—that the call to evangelise *overleaps entirely the bounds of nationality.* In view of sin and its remedy, all mankind form but one nation, and " the field is " literally "THE WORLD." Have I one particle less of responsibility respecting the eternal interests of any human being whom I might possibly reach because we differ in the mere distinction of nationality ? But has this great principle been practically recognised and acted on ? Are we not utterly neglecting innumerable towns and districts almost at our own doors solely because they belong to another nation, for which we should otherwise be in all haste to devote men, and prayer, and money to almost any extent, even if they were five times as distant from our more favoured homes ? Never will the cry for spiritual help from France and other Continental countries be effectually responded to until, before the glance of Christian faithfulness, these arbitrary barriers shall fall, and love for souls shall break through every boundary.

The French Evangelical Churches—what can they do?

"But is not France," you ask, "already in part a Protestant country, so that the duty of giving the Gospel to their neighbours devolves on the French Churches themselves?" A close examination of the relative position of religious and anti-religious parties in France, and of the comparatively few and scattered evangelical communities, could alone conduct to a reliable estimate of what can and what cannot be looked for thence.

We recognise joyfully the gifts both of sanctified intelligence and devout consecration with which our Lord has endowed many in the French Churches. It has been our aim and privilege to have them as our fellow-workers from the beginning. But the unavoidable absorption of a very large part of the time and energy of these pastors in the detail work of their widely dispersed congregations precludes them from personally undertaking aggressive effort on a great scale. Add to this their limited number and the heavy demands made upon the few rich laymen comprised in the evangelical Churches for meeting the heavy claims coming upon them within the limits of the Protestant community, comprising as it does a large section of persons requiring all kinds of material and even spiritual help. There are, indeed, French Societies designed to spread the Gospel at home, and even for sending it to the heathen, worked and sustained by those Churches. Under the former heading are comprised the Société Centrale d'Evangélisation and the Société Evangélique de France. These institutions, seconded by the Mission Intérieure and the Société

Évangélique de Genève (which supports a number of devoted agents in France), are doing an important work for the diffusion of the truth and in planting mission Churches; and we would gladly bespeak for them the offerings and prayers of our readers. And we would put in a similar plea for aid to the evangelistic work of the veteran pastor Armand Delille, and to the kindred enterprises of Miss de Broen, of the Wesleyans, under the direction of the Rev. W. Gibson, and of our Baptist brethren. But in view of the vast field and of the gigantic forces arrayed on the side of Atheism and vice, the utmost that these combined agencies can undertake must be pronounced totally inadequate to meet the pressing need, the imminent crisis. A century would not suffice in which to pervade France with Gospel teachings by means of the existing evangelical communities, unaided from without. What can be looked for, then, in the meanwhile, if we leave our dear French brethren to take the field alone? A century! Who can contemplate without a shudder the condition into which, long ere that century should have run its round, the fair land, unvisited by the one power of healing and of new life, must be plunged?

The Sole Alternative for France—the Gospel or Ruin.

Awake, privileged Christians of Britain and America, to the alternative which hastes towards decision in the sister country. Shall France be deluged with deadly evil, or will you arise and flood it with the Gospel? Shall Voltaire's dark prophecy (at a later date, indeed, than his blasphemous presumption assigned) be terribly fulfilled, or shall the prevalence of a system higher, purer, heaven-born, which he never comprehended, demonstrate that " the weakness of God is stronger than men " ?   There is no possible future for the nation but the one or the other of these.

" Leave the Romanist populations undisturbed rather than lead them to break with the Church of their fore-fathers, and so hazard their drifting away from all re-ligious belief."   Frequent as this lulling cry is in some circles at present, nothing could be more mistaken. No impartial observer can fail to discern that the hold of papal superstition on the convictions of the masses throughout the European continent is essentially on the wane, and must ere long completely fall.   The ascendency may be bolstered up for a time by lures of self-interest or by political intrigue ; but, like all else which will not stand the test of clear insight and impartial investigation, its days are numbered.   We desire to avoid all bitterness ; we gladly recognise the fact that within the Romish pale are to be found many honest and truly devout hearts.   But Romanism, as a system, is utterly incompetent to cope with the anti-religious forces which are abroad.   The emissaries of darkness are busy on every hand.   Infidelity is being sown broadcast by means of political harangues, scientific lectures (so called), Nihilist newspapers, and a whole mass of literature arrayed against the Bible and its Divine Author.   And this relentless crusade goes hand in hand with the sweeping tide of worldliness and immorality, which boldly show themselves in these days, aiming at the very foundations of human society. The theatre, the ball-room, the ribald concert of the wineshop, the racecourse, the gaming-table, the cor-rupting romance, and their thousand concomitants, shall these be suffered to trample on all that is pure

and sober and earnest ? Superstition, hierarchy, pre-
tended miracles, instead of stemming this double tide
of ruin, give to it but freer course, by presenting religion
under distortions from which intelligent thought can
but revolt. The issue must be pronounced as certain—
the handwriting on the wall in characters of fire
announces the impending doom ; the " kingdom " is,
so to speak, on the eve of being " numbered and
finished ; " the unerring " balances " must " find wanting " the godless and degraded mass, unless the
Redeemer of mankind, the riches of forgiving love,
be displayed before the people, unless those who would
save a nation from destruction haste to the rescue, and,
now that " the enemy is coming in like a flood,"
invoke, by consecrated effort and prevailing prayer,
" the Spirit of the Lord " to " lift up against him " the
all-victorious " standard."

The Open Door.

" France has rejected the Gospel ; her day of grace
is ended." Such is another estimate of the case, which
leads many to fold their hands, and look, almost
unmoved, on the advancing tide of desolation. Is it
so ? We could accept this reasoning *if the people now
living in France had individually rejected the Gospel.*
But, in view of the incontrovertible fact that the vast
majority of them have *never had opportunity* to reject the
Divine message, because it has never been borne to them
in its purity, this plea for inaction falls to the ground.

Can any enlightened observer contemplate the
masses, the hundreds of thousands, in Paris itself
who, up to this day, have literally never had a Bible
in their hand, nor have come once within the sound of

the preaching of justification by faith, and say, "These persons have sinned away their day of grace"? And it is not, at least in the vast majority of cases, that they have *refused* to read or to hear. The fact is that neither the Book nor the preacher have ever been brought under their notice. And, after fifteen years of close observation, we affirm that very many *are willing* both to read and to hear when the opportunity is at length presented to them.

But we would not conceal the immense obstacles to Gospel-prevalence which the actual state of the masses of the French people interposes. We dare not say that conscience is tender; far otherwise, alas! A vast work remains to be effected in the *awakening* of the inward monitor. The entire tendency of Romish practices and teachings through a succession of centuries has been to lull conscience into a deep sleep. True insight of sin as heart-rebellion against our heavenly Father is rare indeed. And the hiding of the Bible from view, its becoming *lost sight of*, to an extent hardly credible, through the direct and indirect consequences of Romish prohibition, has been a major cause in producing extremely distorted ideas of religion.

Here and there we find, even among those devotedly attached to Romanism, intelligent observers who deeply feel the need of bringing the "heart-discerning Word of God" out of its long concealment. No testimony to the actual and prevailing *oblivion* of the Book in France could surpass that borne, unconsciously perhaps, by the utterances of such men. Here is one. A gentleman, high in the legal profession in Paris, on occasion of arranging recently the deed of a mission-hall, inquired from me as to our purpose in opening it.

On receiving my reply, he said, with heartfelt emphasis, "Sir, do all in your power to persuade my fellow-countrymen to READ THE BIBLE. If you can induce them to do that, you will bring to France the only power which can save us from decadence and ruin." After attending the opening meeting in that hall, this notary sought me out, and, grasping both my hands in the characteristic French manner, said, "I, a Roman Catholic, desire to assure you of my entire sympathy, my fervent wish for your success." Such a testimony, coming from such a source, may well encourage the directors of the noble work the British and Foreign Bible Society and those of kindred institutions to redouble their efforts to diffuse throughout the land the bread of eternal life!

Throughout the fifteen years' history of our work, we have been constantly meeting with surprising examples of the prevailing inaction, the *deadness* of conscience. Persons who have long attended the meetings with manifest interest, listening to the most faithful and searching addresses, have often amazed us, when closely questioned, by their continued want of spiritual insight, their remaining blindness to the evil of the heart and its remedy. A few years ago, a stalwart and morally upright workman, in the meridian of life, pained the Rev. G. T. Dodds by saying to him, after many an effort had been put forth to awaken him to his state as a sinner, "I admire and delight in the meetings, but you are always speaking to sinners. For my part, I am no sinner. I have nothing with which to reproach myself. I have never wronged any one." Only a few weeks before my beloved colleague's sudden death, he wrote to me, during my summer recess, to gladden me

with the tidings that this workman of Grenelle had at
last come "out of darkness into marvellous light."
This was one of the latest encouragements granted to
that devoted ambassador of Christ ere he was called to
higher service within the veil. "Fool that I was,"
exclaimed the new convert, "to suppose that I was no
sinner! Now all is changed : I see myself the chief."
Shortly afterwards, at the close of a meeting, the man
and his wife came to me, with tears and deep feeling.
The husband said, "I owe everything, under God, to
that dear friend who has left us. Mr. Dodds was my
father in Christ."* The wife added, "And I owe everything to Lord Radstock," whose words had been
effectual in leading her to decision during some meetings following up the visit of Messrs. Moody and
Sankey to Paris. The wife has since died in the Lord.
The husband remains a bold confessor of Christ,
seeking the eternal welfare of his comrades and
neighbours. His sons, even to the youngest, evidence
the same blessed choice. The sacred vow has surely
been fulfilled in that humble home, "As for me and my
house, we will serve the Lord." But my colleague had
been ready to *despair* of that dead conscience, after the
watchings and appeals of many months. Thus, in
thousands of cases, those who seek to "win souls" in
these spiritually darkened countries are called to long
and prayerful effort. "Line upon line" needs to be given,
with ceaseless prayer for the Divine Spirit's vital ray ;

* The memoir of our late beloved colleague by his father-in-
law, the Rev. Horatius Bonar, D.D., was published by Nisbet
and Co. (London, 1884) : "The Life and Work of the Rev. G.
Theophilus Dodds, Missionary in connection with the McAll
Mission, France."

THE LATE REV. G. THEOPHILUS DODDS.

and the patient worker has to grapple with many a temptation to despond and desist ere the first germ of the new creation appears.

While this is so, there are many scattered among the French nation who are already conscious, more or less distinctly, of a deep want of the inner nature which cannot be satisfied until the tempest-tossed soul has found the haven of the Divine Father's love. The notion formed of this void may be very vague, but there it exists. And wherever this is so, the way is prepared for the pure teachings of Christ. These emphatically are the people to whom we are sent. They may be described as WAITING FOR US—for you, Christians of more favoured lands. Each of them reiterates the cry, " Come over and help us." From among those of them to whom our too limited workings can reach, we are, from time to time, permitted to rejoice over new trophies of grace. There is not one among our hundred stations, not the smallest or least apparently blessed, which we are not permitted hopefully to regard as the birth-place of at least some souls. And, as parents are brought to Christ, their children are gladly placed in our Sabbath-schools, there to imbibe those " words of life " which, through the Holy Spirit's power, shall make them " the salt of the earth " in a coming generation.

Here let me cease to speak, and give place to my colleagues in this enterprise, for whose diversified gifts, devotion, and not less affectionate consideration, I render thanks to Him we alike seek to serve. At the outset Mrs. McAll and I laboured almost alone ; now we are surrounded by a noble band of fellow-workers— pastors, evangelists, theological students, laymen, ladies, Bible-readers—alike in Paris and in the provinces.

But, after fifteen years of imperfect though willing
service in this sacred cause, I am constrained to make
an appeal more importunate than ever to British Christians (my dear friend the Rev. W. W. Newell, jun., will
address similarly the Churches of America) to come
yet more largely and generously to our help. I would
fain bring to my task sanctified powers and rich fruits
of experience, like those of my venerated friend the
Rev. Dr. Horatius Bonar, whose pleadings in the
volume to which this is intended simply as a sequel
have been blessed in stirring up a multitude of hearts
to sympathy for France, and have thus, under God,
done more than can ever be estimated at once for the
maintenance and extension of the work.

During the past one or two years, lack of the necessary
funds has compelled us, with unspeakable regret, to
refuse to enter by many an open door. It will be
readily understood that such a work involves a very
large outlay, an outlay, indeed, in consequence of the
much greater cost of rental, living, etc., in France, very
far beyond that which would be required for operations
on the same scale in England. The annual cost of our
mission-halls, containing over 15,000 sittings, along
with the support of those of our workers who (unlike
a few of us) have not independently the means of
support, is unavoidably great. And France demands
that its Christian labourers be speedily multiplied not
tenfold merely—a hundredfold! But this land needs and
asks more than the devotion of money ; personal devotion, that of consecrated lives, is indispensable. Shall
one who has some little claim to speak as a veteran in
the service plead in vain for young and voluntary
recruits ? At this moment, when many are giving

themselves to India, China, Africa, will not some among
our dear young English Christians espouse the work,
as truly a missionary campaign, in this fair land, which
lies waiting at their very doors ?   I pray God to incline
one and another to listen to this appeal, and consecrate
his days and his all in order to strengthen our hands
or those of other labourers in France in the hand-to-
hand struggle to save it from irremediable ruin.

My last and most urgent word shall be a call to join
with us in ceaseless prayer for a blessed revival of God's
work among us, a new baptism of the Holy Ghost to
rest upon us all in France.   I have dwelt equally
upon obstacles and encouragements, upon mountains
to be levelled, principalities of darkness to be met and
vanquished, and upon the great door which the Lord
has opened.   But, on the one hand, were the obstacles
a thousandfold more formidable, they must fall before
God's almighty Spirit ; and, on the other, the widest
open door cannot be successfully entered unless through
His presence and power.   The fields of France may
be white, but we cannot reap them in our own strength.
Ask, then, that our weak faith may be quickened, that
our feeble love for Christ and souls may be inflamed
afresh, that we may be made what He would have us
be as His witnesses.   So that, should we or those who
come after us be privileged, after a few years, to narrate,
for a third time, the history of this enterprise, we may
not only have to speak, as we do to-day, of what our
Lord seems *waiting to accomplish*, but, in view of the
widening triumphs of His grace in France, to record—

"WHAT HATH GOD WROUGHT!"

R. W. McALL.

II

SELECTION OF INCIDENTS.

BEARING DATE SUBSEQUENT TO THE PUBLICATION OF "THE WHITE FIELDS OF FRANCE."

THESE incidents have been chosen as characteristic and suggestive. Several of them are especially valuable as exhibiting the action of the Holy Spirit upon long-deadened conscience.—R. W. McALL.

PARIS AND ITS VICINITY.

"*I shall pray for you.*"

A tall, dignified man shook me warmly by the hand at our Montmartre station. "I know you well, Mr. McAll," he said, "though you cannot recognise me. It is seven years since we last met." In a moment, I felt that his countenance was familiar, though the intervening years had whitened his hair. He reminded me of his attendance, more than seven years before, at our first little meeting-room in Belleville at the very outset of our work. One time, he was much offended because a good German evangelist spoke, and seemed thenceforward to come as a spy, prepared to resent his return. But after that I had remarked his attentive hearing. One Sunday evening, he came to me and said, "In three days, I leave Paris for six or seven years, having an official appointment in New Caledonia. I wish heartily to thank you for these meetings before I go." At the door of the room, I called him back for a moment, simply to say, "My friend, I shall pray for you." Tears started to his eyes, and he was gone. After about seven years, he came to me at another station, saying, "I am the man for whom you promised to pray before I left for New Caledonia. I feel now that you did not forget your promise. Those words seemed to follow me throughout the years, and comforted me when in trouble. I shall be for ever grateful to you for having spoken them." As his stay in Paris was only temporary, he begged me to give him a Bible, inscribed with my name and his, "as a remembrance of the man who promised to pray for him." What a rich recompense for the utterance of those few words !

"*The Letter B in the Spiritual Alphabet.*"

The wife of a painter on porcelain had long attended our Belleville meeting. After a time, her husband, who had been a free-thinker, died. She was very anxious respecting his spiritual state, and there was some hope in his last moments. But, though the widow continued greatly to delight in the meetings, she remained for years without the possession of peace in believing. Our friends often visited her, and found her always full of doubts and sadness. One day, the visitor was surprised to see her all bright and joyous, and inquired the cause. Here are her own quaint words : "Long as I have attended the *réunions*, I had until now reached only the letter A in the alphabet ; now, I believe, I have mastered the letter B." "And what is this letter B?" asked her friend. "Sunday was the most productive day in my little business ; I have just now summoned courage to close my place, and give up, at all costs, my Sunday traffic ; and since doing this, I feel that all is changed." The "letter B" mastered, the "weight laid aside," the monition of conscience at last obeyed, the rest of the "alphabet" soon followed ; light and joy entered her heart. She died, a year or two afterwards, praising God, with her latest breath, for the opening of our mission-room.

"At Eventide it shall be Light."

The family of M. D—— consisted of his wife (a milliner), her assistant, an apprentice, and the apprentice's mother, all Catholics, but not bigoted. They began to attend our Montmartre station about thirteen years ago. The meetings opened to their view a new world ; salvation by free grace soon arrested their attention, and won the hearts, we believe, of all the four. The first symptom of serious interest was the purchase of a Bible by the mother ; it was a new Book to them all. One evening, some weeks after, when I concluded an address by saying, " Go to Jesus ; go to Him as you are ; go to Him this night," she obeyed the call, and has ever since, amidst many afflictions, had peace in believing. One New Year's evening, meeting a pastor and myself at the entrance of the mission-hall, she said, "Oh ! Mr. McAll, I am two years old to-day." The pastor wondered, and she explained that two years before she had commenced to live in Christ. The New Year's Day after their first coming, she said to me, " Everything in our house is completely changed since last New Year's Day ; all is made new." The last of the family to enter our room was the husband, a venerable man, then about eighty years of age, twenty-five or thirty years older than his wife. We commenced a small Friday afternoon prayer-meeting at the station. To our surprise, he was constantly there. He was a very retiring man, but I have seen tears in his eyes, and the warm pressure of his hand told much. Months passed ; they removed to a distance ; infirmities came on the old man ; we missed him from his place. He always welcomed the visits of our friends, but said little. Just as his strength was failing, his lips seemed to be opened. His last words were, " Le Seigneur Jésus vient chercher mon âme" ("The Lord Jesus is come to receive

my spirit "). Up to eighty years of age, he had been quite
ignorant of the Gospel. He received it in the spirit of a
little child. His widow said to me, "Ah, Mr. McAll, my
poor husband suffered much, but he will be one of the bright
jewels in your crown."

A Landlord Brought to Christ in his own Hall.

When we first hired his room, M. —— was cold and
incredulous, a nominal Protestant, but never attending a place
of worship. His wife was strongly attached to Romanism.
After a time, they lost their only daughter. a girl of seventeen
or eighteen, the idol of their heart. This event broke in
upon the father's cold and sceptical state. He began to
attend the meetings. Though a remarkably dignified and
retiring man, I have often seen tears in his eyes. Eventually,
through the addresses of Pastor Bersier, who greatly aids
us at that station, he was led to a humble acceptance of
Christ. His wife also joined him in attendance. The
altered demeanour of our good landlord was very striking ;
his gratitude for the truth he had received found expression
in every look and word. One evening, he gave me a warm
shake of the hand, as I was about to take a journey. A few
days afterwards, on my return, I learned that he was already
laid in the grave. Sudden illness had cut him down at
fifty-eight years of age. To one of our friends visiting her,
the widow said, " Had this occurred before we knew the con-
solations of the Gospel, I could not possibly have borne it.
As it is, I weep because my dear husband is removed, but
I am enabled to say, ' The Lord gave, the Lord hath taken
away ; blessed be the name of the Lord." She and her only
son (since deceased) gave afterwards a practical proof of
their reverence for the Gospel in renewing our lease of their
large hall at a rent little more than half that which was
offered them for another purpose, and still more recently
the widow, in her loneliness, has repeated the sacrifice, and

made the place sure to the Mission so long as we may desire to retain it.

" *Taken in the Net*."

An intelligent young business-man passed by our mission-hall in the Rue de Rivoli, and was invited to enter. Up to that time, to use his own expression, he was a *mondain* (worldling). One of the speakers was advising his hearers to read the Bible. He went away making a promise to himself that he would do so. At first the Book irritated him, and he nearly gave up reading it; but, remembering his resolution, he determined to read it to the end. One evening M. Sainton was speaking on the parable of the net and fishes. He said, " Have you been taken in this net ? " The address was blessed to his decision for Christ. Shortly afterwards he gave his public testimony of having been " taken in this net." In August, when about to leave Paris on a long business journey, he wrote to Mr. Dodds, " I regret much that I shall be deprived for some time of what is to me a very great pleasure,—that of preaching the Gospel of salvation in your meetings. However, I hope that the time spent away from Paris will not be lost." While diligent in business, he has become a zealous Christian worker, especially among the young men of Paris.

" *I believed Nothing, but admired the Speeches*."

We had long noticed in our Rue de Rivoli station a hearer in the prime of life, bearing the marks of intelligence and education. He attended with marked regularity, but always left quickly at the close, so that for months no one could bring him into conversation. At length two of our young evangelists gained his confidence. They found him to be interested and thoughtful, but as yet far from a clear view, and further still from heartfelt acceptance, of the Gospel. Their efforts were blessed in leading him on to a full and avowed decision. The following are, as nearly as we can render them, his own words.

"When I first came into the mission-hall and heard the addresses, I said to myself, 'There is Jesuitism in this.' Soon, however, I became struck with the evident deep conviction of the speakers, and, although I often said to myself, 'That is great nonsense' ["des bêtises"], I yet felt constrained to add, 'It is nonsense extremely well put' ["des bêtises très bien dites"]. I was still a sceptic, but gradually saw there was truth in what was said. You gained my esteem because no attack was made on any person or Church."

The light came slowly and after hard struggling with old traditions. Like many others in France, he was a nominal Catholic, but at heart an unbeliever. Never shall we forget the thrill of joy experienced on first speaking with him after, as a humbled sinner, he had come to the foot of the Cross. All his natural reserve was broken through, and his offer after the French fashion, of both his hands told the love and gratitude of his heart. The happy change had lighted up his countenance with a new expression.

" *Take—read.*"

A young student of one of the great Government colleges entered our new mission-room at Versailles. He was likewise nominally a Catholic, but destitute of all religious conviction. That evening a speaker related the vision of St. Augustine, when he seemed to hear the voice, "Take—read." That very night he sought his neglected Bible (he possessed the De Sacy version), and, for the first time in his life, set himself to read it. "The Word did not return void." The silent perusal awoke deep anxiety in his spirit. The valued friends who help us at that station noticed him, and were enabled to lead him on, after a severe inward conflict, to peace in believing. His college course coming to a close, he desired, before returning to his widowed mother in a distant town, not only to join with the Protestant Church at the Lord's Table, but in our mission room, where his new life had commenced, to bear a public testimony for his Saviour. This was done with touching humility, yet with firmness, and evidently made a deep impression upon the hearers, among whom were several of his fellow-students.

The Old Soldier of Les Invalides.

A lady visitor went to the Hospice Neckar to visit a man who had regularly attended our little mission-hall, Rue de la Comète, for more than a year. Alas! bed No. 10 had received another patient; M. C—— lay in his coffin in the garden below, awaiting the honours accorded him, as an army veteran, of a military escort to his last resting-place. He had been suddenly summoned to meet the great Captain. The battle was over, and the victory won! M. C—— had served in the Franco-German war, had been wounded and made prisoner during the siege of Strasburg. His only little girl died of fright during the bombardment. Restored, after peace was signed, to his country, he began to hunger after something which superstition and external forms could not give. An acquaintance, a shoemaker, advised him to go to our little hall, and there he was ever after to be seen in his place until laid aside by sickness. The addresses, our friendly visits, and the daily study of the big Bible he had borrowed from an Alsatian comrade, opened his eyes to the truth. There he found, as he expressed it, "the justification unto life, through Jesus, and without works." Being at leisure, he spent hours in turning over his Bible—his "treasure" he termed it—marking with numerous bits of paper the passages that struck him, or on which he wanted further light. He spent the little cash he could save from his small pension in buying little books elucidating the Scriptures.

One day, he said to his visitor, " Madam, I have learned two prayers." Standing up, with hands folded behind him like a child, he repeated, not in Latin, but in his native tongue, the Apostles' Creed and the Lord's Prayer. When he came to the last clause, " Thine is the kingdom," etc., he burst into tears, exclaiming, " Oh, it is too magnificent ! too magnificent ! My God, Thou art glorious, and—Thou carest for ME ! "

" It is written," was one of his favourite expressions, and, to his simple faith, an unanswerable argument. " Look you, madam," he would say, "this is my regulation-book [laying his hand firmly on the Bible]. What I find here, I accept and obey. What I find not here [with a decisive wave of the hand], I reject."

Six months before his death, he had openly declared, in an after-meeting, his acceptance of the Gospel, and shortly after was admitted a member of M. Paumier's Church. With what joy he looked forward to the communion season ! " To-morrow is *the great day*, sister. To-morrow I shall sit down at the Lord's Table. Will you be there, sister ? "

After bearing a faithful testimony among his friends and in the hospital, where his fellow-patients described him as "a man of great faith and well-taught," he has fallen asleep in Jesus till called to the marriage-supper of the Lamb.

The Itinerant Knife-grinder.

One of the patients of our Grenelle dispensary died. Here is his touching history. He came to the dispensary early in the spring, wretched in all respects, in poverty, sickness, ignorance of all Divine things, despair. He was cared for in every sense, but seemed spiritually to remain in total darkness. Among other things, a copy of one of the Gospels was given to him. After about a month he disappeared. Then one of our friends was sent for to his wretched lodging. He learned that, the poor knife-grinder having become more grievously ill, he had been taken to a neighbouring hospital. When it became evident to the "Sisters" that death was near, they insisted on his receiving the visit of a Romish priest. This he refused, saying that he desired to see "the gentleman of the dispensary." As he persisted in this, he was sent back from the hospital to his miserable abode. There "the gentleman of the dispensary" found him, but how changed! Disease had made rapid strides ; evidently he had not many hours to live. But what a transformation !—the gloom which had before settled on his countenance replaced by an expression of peace and even joy ; the almost heathen darkness exchanged for a humble belief in his Saviour. In the hospital, bereft of every other teacher, God's Spirit had opened to him the truth in the little Gospel he had carried with him there. Here are his very words, spoken to our friend : "Now I am fully convinced that we can be justified only by the meritorious death of Christ." The day following, he died. His wife said that, to the last, he was engaged almost constantly in prayer and repeating the name of Jesus. On occasion of his funeral, M. Vallette, the devoted Lutheran pastor, who himself died shortly afterwards, said to the company of workmen and neighbours assembled in his church, "Now we have the proof before our own eyes that the pure truth of Christ can bring new life to a Parisian workman when sinking in death."

Losing a Purse to Find a Saviour.

About New Year's Day, 1884, a lady of some thirty-five or forty years of age, with her two children (a thoughtful-looking boy of about twelve and his sister), entered the Salle Philadelphie one week evening. We shall not forget the expression of the lady's countenance, nor that of the boy. Surprise and intense interest were written on their features.

They evidently listened for every accent of the hymns and for every word of the preaching and prayer.

Here is their history, as we afterwards learned it, and the mode in which they were led (by chance) to enter. The lady, a Russian of St. Petersburg, had lost her husband, in the prime of life, eight years before. The boy's health failing, she had been ordered by the doctors to take him to Nice, in the south of France. Her small means were well-nigh exhausted. But the child's health was restored, and she was hastening to return to her home in St. Petersburg. Passing through Paris *en route*, she arrived late at night, intending to hurry on next morning. She discovered that her travelling bag had been robbed on the railway, and she was thus detained, much against her will, in the foreign city, and left there without resources, until telegraphic messages should have reached St. Petersburg, and money could arrive.

She accordingly—the next evening, I believe—walked out from her hotel with the two children to pass the time. They were near the great church of La Madeleine. Passing along the street, they heard the sound of music and singing. " Oh, mamma," cried the children, " there is a concert ; let us go in." " I regret that I cannot take you to hear the music, but you know our money has not yet come from St. Petersburg." So they all turned away, when, in the same moment, a very poor man came up to the door—it was that of the Salle Philadelphie—and our friend who stood there to invite the passers-by said to him, " Enter, my friend. It is free. There is nothing to pay." The words, intended only for the poor man, fell on the Russian lady's ear. " We can go in," she said to her children ; " there is nothing to pay."

At the close of the meeting, one of our Christian ladies, who had remarked the intense listening of the little group, went up and kindly spoke to the lady. With deep feeling, she replied, "Madam, never did I hear anything like this in my country; no one ever told me these blessed things. I shall come here every night until I return to Russia." She did so. She procured a Bible, and for the first time in her life, read it with her children. The boy in particular set himself to study God's Book. When they arrived at any difficulty, he would say, "Mamma, have you forgotten that we had the answer to that question in such and such a passage which we were reading the other day?" and then he would quote the text.

The same lady went to visit the new-comer. At the close, prayer was proposed, and that exercise completely broke her down. It was so new and wonderful to one who all her life had been accustomed to the ritualistic formalism of the Greek Church. One time our friend said to her, in order to ascertain clearly her state of mind, "You know, madam, that a sudden call might summon you into eternity. If this were the case—if it should arrive to-night —whither would you go?" The other paused, then took both the hands of her questioner, and replied, "If, in order to go to heaven, it is enough to believe in Jesus Christ and love Him, I should go there."

In due time she returned to her own country. Thence she sent to our friends a touching account of her first Sabbath in her old home, and her attendance on the simple Gospel meetings held in St. Petersburg, closing with the expression of boundless gratitude to God that she had ever been invited to the "chère Salle Philadelphie." We had the happiness of giving her introductions to valued Christian friends in her own city. Since then it seems that she has been sorely persecuted by her family connections, but manifests firmness in confessing Christ.

"*Poorer in Pocket, Rich in Heart.*"

Our colleague the Rev. S. R. Brown writes :—"One

evening I went to the Salle New York, Rue de Rivoli, and found a large *queue* formed at the door waiting to go in, so I walked round the houses, and was accosted by three persons also waiting the opening of the doors. ' Oh, c'est Monsieur,' said one ; ' we have been looking for you, and had I known your address, we should have come to see you.' There was something so warm, so cordial in my reception, that it caused me to say, ' I have not the pleasure of remembering you.'

" ' Oh ! ' she said, ' it was last Wednesday I resolved to be of your religion ; since then I have been so happy, and I wanted to speak to you about it.'

" The *queue* had disappeared at the door, and eight o'clock struck, so, receiving her address, we entered the meeting joyful at the good news, waiting to pay her a visit on the next day, when we were introduced to her husband, a gentleman of colour, whom we had noticed at the meeting.

" Let us give her own story as illustrating God's work. They had come from Montevideo, South America, to form in Paris a financial enterprise for that town, hoping to return before the winter. One evening they were walking about in the Square St. Jacques, when they made the acquaintance of two German maids, who pressed her to come to the meeting. The husband yielded, saying, ' It will pass an hour; let us go.' They found it pleasant from its novelty, but, the following evening, the story of Christ's dying on the Cross was told ; the hymns were all about the Cross. ' I had never heard Jesus spoken about in this wise,' she said, ' my heart was touched, and I cried. So I got a Bible, and began to read and pray from my heart. Then on Wednesday I was thinking, ought I to leave my religion ? When I went to the meeting, and the address was on the text, " How long halt ye between two opinions ? " as the speaker proceeded, I could hesitate no longer. I resolved to serve God, and to trust alone in the sacrifice of Jesus and His mediation, and then I was filled with joy.' She began to weep. Her outward tears were a witness of her inward joy. She added, 'We are on the eve of returning to America.' We knelt down in their lodging to praise God that He had revealed in her His Son Jesus, and to pray that the husband might be made partaker of the same faith. Her progress has been rapid; and a few weeks afterwards she expressed a wish to go to the Lord's Table. I was surprised to find her views so clear, so spiritual—surely she was taught of the Spirit—and her German friend had helped her in the study of the Bible. On the first Sabbath in October she was received as a member of the Lutheran Church, Rue des Billettes.

"The wife soon became anxious for the salvation of her husband; she wanted him to share her faith, to be a partaker of her joy; and God has given to her the desire of her heart. On Sunday, the 16th of December, she spoke at our fraternal meeting, giving public testimony to the great change wrought within her, and praising God for what He had done. At the close of the meeting she requested that prayer should be offered for herself and husband at our special service at the Oratoire that night.

"At the close of the service she came to me with a face radiant, as I have seldom seen, with inward joy. Her husband was with her. 'My husband is decided, he is convinced, he has given himself; *n'est-ce pas, mon ami?*'

"To this appeal he answered, with quivering lips and moistened eyes, 'Oh, yes! thank God!'

"'Our financial loss has been great,' said the wife, 'but no material loss can be compared with our spiritual gain; no sacrifice too great, in view of what we have found in Paris.'

"Up to the time of leaving Paris, they both gave clear evidence of genuine attachment to the Saviour. On Aug.

24th, 1884, we bade them farewell in the *réunion*, Rue St. Honoré, commending them to God, with prayer that they might be made a blessing in their distant home. They were greatly moved; we too felt much on taking their hands, probably for the last time on earth. The wife said, 'My husband was later in setting out, but he has gone before me now.' So they left Paris, to use their own expression, 'poorer in pocket, but *rich* in heart.'"

Two Saviours.

One night, a workman at Grenelle after-meeting, now a devoted and active Christian, told a most pointed story of his own life. "I have had two saviours," he said. "The first was after the Commune. I was taken and accused as a Communist, and, without any form of trial, was marched to instant death. In my own eyes I was a dead man. Marching across the Champ de Mars, we met an officer, who touched me, and said to the soldiers, 'What are you doing with that man there? I answer for him; he is an honest man; let him go.' They let me go. This man was my saviour. I did not know then that I was in danger of another death, that my sin had condemned me before God. Years after, I found it out, and I was in despair. I could see no way to be saved. Then Jesus Christ passed by, and said, 'This man —I answer for him.' And a second time I was saved."

The Saviour Found at Eighty-five Years of Age.

The Salle Philadelphie is chiefly frequented by well-to-do persons, but attracts occasionally the very poor. We well remember noticing a very aged woman, characteristic in her peasant dress and shrivelled countenance, who began attendance some years ago. Literally she has rarely missed the meeting a single evening since. It has become not only her delight, but, one might say, her very life.

Here is her simple history. In her young days, sixty or seventy years ago, meetings were held for the people, in the middle of Paris, by a curé or abbé of the Romish Church. Everything was gratuitous. There were French hymns sung, and addresses also were made in French. She had attended these meetings and taken great delight in them, when they were discontinued.

She married, and went to reside with her husband at Oran, in Algeria. After a few years he died. She removed to Paris, and there, in a very humble position, lived a struggling life for many, many years. She remained nominally a Romanist, but longed for the meetings of old, and the hymns in her own language.

At length she vaguely overheard, on the staircase of the large old house in a garret of which she lodges, a conversation by persons unknown to her respecting " meetings in the centre of Paris, free for all, in which hymns were sung in French." She inquired of a policeman, and he directed her to the Salle Philadelphie.

From the first night of her coming her heart was touched. All was a new discovery to her ; she had never heard the pure Gospel message before. Through listening constantly to the addresses, and through conversation with our friends (though she cannot read), she has gained, at eighty-five years of age, a clear view of the foundation of the sinner's hope. For example, when urged by neighbours or relatives to return to the confessional, she replied, " What an idea to attempt to make any sacrifice to God, when Jesus has Himself offered for us the only sacrifice that is of any worth!" She has become a member of one of the Free Churches. She still lives in her small garret, three yards square, in the sixth story, with "only a crust ; " but she avows herself quite happy, waiting for the end.

How many of these " hidden ones " may there be in this vast city longing for half a century to be met on their lonely

way by the message of Heaven's love in sweet hymns or the
uttered words of life !

" What is that large Book you read from ?"

The following history is from the pen of our colleague
the Rev. S. R. Brown :—"A landed proprietor used to come
yearly to Paris, to enjoy its pleasures, attending the theatre
every alternate night for six months. In January, 1885, he
again came back to Paris from his country home, to worship
the goddess of pleasure. When sauntering along the Great
Boulevard he was accosted by an English gentleman, Mr.
Soltau, who invited him to a 'Conférence Gratuite sur
l'Evangile.' He went in. It was our hall of Boulevard
Bonne Nouvelle, Salle Baltimore. A dignified but kind
American lady handed him a hymn-book, and pointed to
a chair. The attention flattered him, and he said to himself, 'She is a lady all over.' The preacher was Pastor
Théodore Monod. The gentleman was pleased, and came
again ; but the distance was great from his house. and he
inquired of the lady who gave him a tract on going out if
any such gathering existed nearer his home, and was told
there was one at Batignolles. It was thus we met at Salle
Cleveland. The president read from a large book ; the
words were new to him ; he had never heard them before.
How beautiful ! 'What book is that you read from, sir ?'
'The Bible ! or what we call "La Parole de Dieu."' 'The
Bible ! Could you lend it me for a week ? I will bring it
back. I never heard these words before !' 'Oh,' replied
the preacher, 'I will give you a Gospel,' and handed him
the Gospel of John. He thanked him, gave his card, and
went away. Next Tuesday he returned the Gospel, saying,
'That is not the book you read from ; cannot you lend me
THE BOOK ?' 'Certainly,' was the answer ; so I gave him
a copy. It was small, and he found out where to buy one,
and went and bought a large Bible for himself. 'Strange,'

he said, ' I never saw this book before, and since hearing
you read it I went to three booksellers in Batignolles, intending to buy it ; but they could neither supply it nor tell
me where to procure one. Then I sent my wife round,
hoping she might succeed, and she came back with this
statement : " It was a bad book, a forbidden book, and only
used by priests and pastors." * So I was afraid I could not
get it. Now I shall read it, measure and weigh every
word.' He became a regular attendant at our meetings,
and asked many questions about what he heard and read.
One evening he was deeply impressed, and said, ' I have
learned more in one meeting than from seven years of
philosophy taught me by a learned Jesuit father.' Progress
was slow; the sun had risen, but the day was long in
breaking; clouds gathered, unbelief held fast, and difficulties cropped up on every side.

" 'Why did not the rulers believe on Him if miracles were
wrought? Why did not the Pharisees acknowledge their
Messiah?' So he found in the Bible 'things hard to be
understood,' nor could he then believe the Incarnation.
For God to become Man was *un abaissement*, a degradation
of the Deity he could not accept.

" The time approached for his return into the country, and
he was an inquirer, not yet a Christian ; a seeker, not
saved. So I prepared a special address on the words, ' I
thank Thee, O Father, that Thou hast hid these things from
the wise and prudent, and hast *revealed* them unto the
simple.' We went to the meeting as usual. Our friend sat
in his seat, Mr. McAll presided, and a strange preacher came.

" ' I shall not ask you to speak first,' said our president,
' but M. le Pasteur.'

---

* This incident exhibits the great need and value of the Dépôts
Bibliques recently opened, with the aid of the British and Foreign
Bible Society, on the street fronts of several of our stations in Paris
and in the provinces.

" ' Very well.'

" Mr. McAll, knowing nothing of my purpose, read Luke x., the very chapter containing my text ; and, strange to say, the new preacher took my text and preached my intended sermon ! Wonderful coincidence ! but not rare in Gospel work. I added a few words, and we went towards the station, my friend accompanying us.

" ' What a conspiracy ! ' he said. ' You three have put your heads together to preach to me.'

" ' No,' was the answer ; ' the preacher is a stranger to me, and does not know you.'

" ' But you told him all about me ? '

" ' *Au contraire*, we have never spoken to each other.'

" ' But you meant your discourse for me ? '

" ' Yes ; prepared on purpose to meet your difficulties ; but no one except myself knew you.'

" ' *Tiens !* it is strange ; ' and he began to muse. So we said no more. The light had penetrated ; it was day-dawn.

" As the time drew near for his departure, he was anxious I should visit him in his pleasant country home to preach to the crofters of his native village, but most of all that we might ponder over the Word of God. He wrote, ' Do come ; I cannot walk alone ; I need to have many things explained.' So I went, and, sitting under his nut trees, we read of Jesus predicted in the Old Testament, going through Adolphe Monod's book, ' Lucile ; ou, La Lecture de la Bible,' and reading all that the prophets wrote of Him. We walked together one day through a wood. The light anon broke through the trees and lay in bands of golden hue across our path. We stood long to converse, and I had ceased to speak, when he said, ' I never heard these things before. All so new. I never saw a Bible before. I went to Paris for pleasure, a Deist, believing nothing. Death, I thought, was annihilation ; religion useful, but false ; and

Jesus a myth. You have taught me that God became Man. I have learned from Adolphe Monod's book that we need a sacrifice to cleanse away our sin. *Now I believe in Jesus Christ !* '

" He was anxious that others should know that he was a new man, and had begun to fashion his life after the teaching of the Gospel as he had heard it in Paris, and especially according to the words, ' Love your enemies,' ' Overcome evil with good.'

" On the Sunday he gathered all his neighbours together in his crofter's kitchen. The large chair of the time of Louis XV. was taken in for the preacher, and all the village met to hear the Word. He said, ' I am anxious that my people should hear the Gospel. Now, don't preach a grand sermon to them, for they won't understand you. But I want you to talk to them about the Lord Jesus Christ. Tell them how He, the great God, became a Servant, and that they may all become citizens of heaven.' Having from a full heart told me what to preach, and how, we went in. The room was packed. He acted ' as if Mr. McAll,' presiding, selecting and reading the third chapter of John's Gospel. Then he introduced me ; and for fifty minutes I told the old, old story of Jesus, who came to save the lost. The meeting over, we went into his garden, and sat under the nut trees. Then he said :

" ' I am glad my enemy was there ; I want to see him converted. He is a bad man.'

" ' Was I simple enough ? ' I asked.

" ' No,' he answered. ' Why do you use such hard words to these peasants ? ' But he was little disposed to complain. ' To-day,' he said, ' you have broken the silence of two hundred years. Never since the revocation of the Edict of Nantes has the Gospel been preached in these parts ; and to-day you have dropped some living germs that will live and spread. And in years to come the children

4

will talk of the service in the crofter's kitchen. I am so
glad my enemy was there ! '

"I asked him, ' From your experience, what advice can
you give as to the best subjects most likely to lead a
Parisian to God ? '

" ' Tell them,' he said with animation, ' " I thank Thee, O
Father, that Thou hast hid these things from the wise and
prudent [from Pharisee and Sadducee], and hast revealed
them unto the simple." '

"So it has pleased God to reveal His Son to this *bourgeois ;*
and he is now circulating and even writing tracts, and
seeking to lead others into the way of righteousness."

An English Working Men's Mission to French "*Ouvriers.*"

The Rev. S. H. Anderson writes :—" Creil is one of the
principal stations on the main line between Paris and
Boulogne. From its vicinity, railways stretch north, south,
east, and west, indeed in six different directions across the
country. Close to it are the extensive foundries of Montataire ; and the blaze of furnaces lights up the skies as one
walks from the station to the meeting-place. When we
think of the thousands of workmen and their families settled
in this neighbourhood, we cannot but thank God for having
led the McAll Mission to establish itself in this centre.
The work was commenced on the 21st of April, 1885, and
ever since I and my colleagues go thither from Paris by
turns each Wednesday night.

" On my way from the station I distribute tracts, and invite
the groups of workmen going home and others to the
'Conférences' held every Wednesday evening at eight
o'clock in the Englishmen's Dining Room, or 'Salle à
Manger des Anglais de Saxby et Farmer.' All the tracts
are thankfully received in the shops and on the road, almost
every person addressed knowing of the meetings, several

saying, 'Thank you ; we have been there already, and shall go again.'

" Beautiful it is to see British workmen witnessing for God, and glorifying Christ in trying to do good to the French among whom, for the present, their lot is cast. But it is not among the French alone that the influence of the work encouraged by these few English Christians is felt, for Flemish and Dutch workmen settled in the neighbourhood also frequent the meetings.

"Often there is no sitting room left. Frequently nearly two hundred are present, while groups of timid listeners persist in standing outside in the cold.

" The interest that the English workmen and their wives take in this work is admirable. The principles of the Evangelical Alliance practised so thoroughly in the McAll Mission are readily seen here. One is a Baptist, another a Congregationalist, a third belongs to the Free Church of Scotland, and usually a young lady belonging to the Church of England plays the harmonium. A group of ladies and children belonging to the little English colony heartily join in the singing, doing their best with the translated Sankey's hymns and others, so as to lead and teach the French to praise the Lord. One meets here with the same rapt attention that prevails in any of the long-established McAll meetings, and, as elsewhere, many with tearful eyes, or a beaming countenance and a hard grip of the hand, pass out of the room.

" A poor workman came forward and said, as he heartily grasped my hand, ' I also am a child of God, sir.' He added, ' I have rest now. Two years ago I did not know what it was.'

" ' It cannot be otherwise,' I said, ' for Christ's words are, " Come unto Me, and I will give you rest." '

" ' And with that rest,' continued my friend, ' one can better endure the trials of life.'

"A bright fair-haired girl of fourteen earned only a few sous per week, doing scavenger's work. She came one day with a little heap of pence (her hard savings) to purchase a Bible, requesting to be taught to read every evening, so that she might read the Bible for herself. The daughter of our zealous Scotch friend readily undertook this duty.

"One of our zealous English friends said to me, 'I never thought, when I first came to Creil, that I should see the day when French workmen would sing Gospel hymns while employed in the workshop. Now, they tell us, it is a frequent occurrence. The children also may be heard singing them in the cottages.'"

An Eloquent Carpet.

One Monday evening, on arriving at the hall of Boulevard Barbès (Salle Boston), Mr. McAll was taken by surprise on being presented with a beautiful drawing-room carpet, accompanied with ornamental needle-book and fresh flowers offered to Mrs. McAll, the whole as a "testimonial of affection and gratitude" on the part of the regular attendants of the station. The names were all inscribed on a document prepared for the purpose. This evidence of regard was deeply touching, after nearly fourteen years, during which Mr. McAll had regularly conducted that Monday meeting, Mrs. McAll being all the time organist. Pastor Bersier followed with a most kind and warm-hearted address. The affectionate feeling—like that of a family— prevailing in this large station is, we are assured, the product of the love of Christ shed abroad in many hearts.

A few weeks afterwards, the poor working people of the same station presented an elegantly bound volume to Pastor Bersier, in token of gratitude for his long-continued and most valuable help in the meetings. On this occasion, the fourteenth anniversary of the opening of the first little room in the quarter, Mr. McAll stated the belief that, during the interval, as many had received the Gospel there as the entire company—three hundred or more—then assembled. A large number of these had died in the Lord.

Fraternal Societies.

Few experiences would be more impressive than to find one's self, at a stone's throw from the incessant whirl of the Great Boulevard, in the side-room of our mission-hall of Boulevard Bonne Nouvelle (Salle Baltimore), surrounded by the numerous members of the fraternal Society gathered in that station, and in so many others. The seriousness, the sympathy pervading the company of eighty or a hundred persons who have remained after the nightly meeting of nearly three hundred has dispersed, tells irresistibly of a work of grace and of the power of the Divine Spirit to reach the heart in the very vortex of ungodly Paris. We have been there frequently when, in response to the invitation of the much-loved president, M. Saillens, simple and touching personal testimonies have been given, and prayers have been offered, sometimes in broken accents, by those who never previously opened their lips in prayer before others. On a recent Sabbath evening in this hall, where, at the outset, the opposition of surrounding immorality and anti-religion had to be severely felt, at least two hundred and fifty persons remained, mostly men, after the general assembly had been dismissed, to hear a statement, in the name of this fraternal Society, from a tradesman, one of its members. This statement was an earnest appeal from those who had received Christ in the station to their fellow-hearers to aid, according to their ability, in removing the financial difficulties resting at the time on the Mission. In profound silence, the whole company heard this man, in life's prime, publicly declare that he himself was one of those who, through attendance on the meetings there, had "passed from death unto life."

Through the generosity of friends in Edinburgh, we have this year been enabled to open two free dispensaries in Paris : at our stations of Les Ternes (Salle Beach) and Gare d'Ivry (Salle Yulee de Florida). The great blessing attending Miss de Broen's medical mission in Belleville, of which Dr. Colin Macrae is the physician, suggested the importance of extending the same kind of effort to other needy districts. Our medical missionary is Dr. Daniel Elie Anderson, and already much good has attended his labours. The Gare d'Ivry, in particular, is one of the most crowded and destitute quarters of Paris. It is a touching spectacle to see the large group of poor and suffering people assembled when the dispensary is opened, and especially the interest and emotion with which they join in the religious exercises. One of the patients, on being restored to health, begged permission to continue attendance, in order not to miss the simple worship which she had found so precious. Our director, Dr. Hastings Burroughs, has a similar and very efficient free dispensary in connection with the Branch Mission at St. Etienne.

Miss Ritchie, a lady who disinterestedly renders valuable aid in the work of the dispensaries, writes :—" The other night, at our station of Les Ternes, a neighbouring pastor remarked to me, 'There is a change in the audience here which I do not quite understand. Formerly it had the aspect of respectability and chapel-going, but whence do these other people come who have listened with such marked attention?' 'Oh,' I said, 'these are patients of the dispensary, who have discovered that they have other diseases to be healed than those of the body.' The same experience meets us in visiting among the patients. Their hearts being already softened by practical sympathy, they listen with conviction to the Word of God read to them.

Yesterday, after reading to a woman who was very ill, several neighbours being also present, of the gift of God as for 'whosoever will,' she exclaimed, ' Ah, madam, your religion is for the poor and the unfortunate.' Another, with an incurable disease, was longing for the return of Dr. Anderson (absent for needed rest), because she thought he could keep her alive until she should be more prepared to die. Now all fear is taken away, and she is resting on the one sure foundation. Above fifty addresses of patients living near Salle Beach have been taken in charge by four ladies ; so, in ploughing up this fallow ground, we know not how many jewels may be claimed from it by the Lord of hosts when He makes up His own. The confidence in Dr. Anderson's skill is unbounded, and much true gratitude is evidenced."

THE DEPARTMENTS OF FRANCE.

LYONS.

"It will help me to Heat my Furnace."

On occasion of opening our first mission-room in Lyons, that of La Guillotière, in the midst of a dense and degraded population, a stoker came in, with his black face and in his working clothes. He listened, with rapt attention, to the close. On leaving, he said to one of our friends, "Never in my life have I heard the truth thus explained ; this is what I want." The next meeting-night he came neatly dressed and with a clean face, and thenceforward became a constant attendant. Here is a literal translation of some of his words : "I know always that there is something here [laying his hand on his heart] which cannot die, but never before had this been so well explained to me. I shall think of it during the week, and that will help me to heat my furnace." A year and a half afterwards, paying a second visit to Lyons, I went to the same station, and the stoker

came forward, with a beaming countenance, to tell me that
he should be eternally grateful for the opening of that
mission-room.

" I came here to get Happiness, and I get only Misery."

In 1883, Pastor Duchemin, then director of our Lyons
branch, wrote :—"In the mission-room of La Guillotière, a
most populous and spiritually destitute district of the town,
I had often noticed a well-dressed and evidently respectable
workman, with his wife and two children. He always took
his place immediately in front of me, and fixed his eye on
the speaker with a wonderful intensity. A few weeks ago,
he came up to me at the close of a meeting and said, ' I
have come to say adieu.'

" ' Oh, you are going away ? '

" ' No, sir ; but you see me here to-night for the last time.'

" ' On what account ? '

" ' I came here to get good, and I get only misery.'

" ' Misery ! but how ? '

" ' Yes ; before I began to attend I was calm, but what I
hear troubles me. I see my sin, which becomes black,
black, which mounts, mounts, and chokes me.'

" These were his very words. They took me by surprise ;
I was moved, and under the impulse of the emotion, I
threw my arms round him.

" ' Oh, my friend,' I cried, ' return ! Do you not perceive
that it is God who is speaking to you ? Listen to Him,
instead of withstanding Him and hardening your heart
against Him. Do you not know that Jesus Christ is come
to heal those who feel themselves sick, to save those who
feel themselves lost ? Soon you will know Him better, and
He will give you His peace. Promise me to return.'

" He promised. I could not then urge him further. The
true sense of sin is so rare in our poor country that it is
necessary to guard any adverse breath that might quench

the spark. The Holy Spirit was working in this soul, and I felt I must for the time leave it with Him, persuaded that He would, in His own time, open the man's eyes to see the infinite mercy of God. Meanwhile, I bore him on my heart in prayer.

"A fortnight after, I again visited that station, and this man sat before me, his eye fixed on me like a gimlet ready to run me through. I spoke of the first and second Adam, —of the position of each hearer, through the first Adam, as in a state of suffering, wretchedness, and sin; and of the heritage of a new humanity in the second Adam through the Spirit, reconciled, received in grace, newly created by Him, prepared for new obedience, believing, hoping, living, find-ing even in suffering the token of Fatherly love; and I closed by the line of one of our hymns—

The tempest itself will guide us into port.

"I was greatly moved, as was the entire assembly. I felt that what I was saying for one of my hearers went home to and impressed them all. The instant the meeting was over, the man came to me, took both my hands (very expressive in France—often done by a new convert when first greeting those who helped him to find the Saviour), and said, 'I have understood to-night what I never understood before : that Jesus Christ *is a Saviour.* Hitherto that was for me only a word, a form of speech; now I *see Him as such.*'

"I said, 'You need to go one step further; do you under-stand that He is *your* Saviour?'

"He reflected a moment, then said, 'Not yet.'

"'Then ask of Him to make you understand that also.'

"The subsequent history of this workman gave every ground to recognise a genuine work of grace in his heart."

A Season of Revival.

With reference to the progress of the work at Lyons, Major Colquhoun, its director, thus writes at the close of 1885 :—

" With encouragements here and there during the whole course of the year, signs that the Lord was blessing us, and the firm assurance of 'more to follow,' we saw the cultivation of the field progress, the undergrowth and withered branches removed one by one, and the soil opened up to the sun. On the 1st of November, with the aid of our dear brother Mr. Vernier, of Valence, we commenced in all the *salles* a series of special meetings, which were immediately blessed to the conversion of souls. Many of these testified to having been anxiously waiting for years without discovering how to take hold of the Lord Jesus by faith. What heart-stirring scenes we soon witnessed in the *salles* of Lyons!—whole families giving themselves in their individual members to the Lord. One instance of father, mother, two daughters, son, and cousin, being converted, and immediately testifying to their change of heart. Another, of father, mother, two sons, and young daughter, all brought in, through the decision and testimony of the little girl last named. Yet another, of father, mother, grandfather, and grandmother—an old couple of over seventy—with their little granddaughter, all testifying for the Lord Jesus. Many cases of members of families, men and women, young girls and lads, receiving Christ as their Saviour.

" Sufficient to say, that, as the outcome, we have organised on Sabbath afternoons a special meeting for those who declare they have given themselves to the Lord Jesus. The meeting is held in our central *salle.* Many converts are quite unable to come in from the outlying quarters of the city,— the winter has been a severe one, with much rain, snow, and ice,—but already *one hundred and twelve* are inscribed on the list, with an average attendance of about sixty. The assemblage is a most joyful one; two hours quickly pass in praise, exhortation, testimony, and prayer. It is an open meeting, intended to be conducted by the converts themselves. New cases of conversion are occurring every week.

Our friend and brother Mr. Vernier, who has been the means of bringing this great blessing to us, is much beloved in consequence."

ST. ETIENNE.

A Day of Ingathering to the Church.

In January, 1883, a most impressive meeting was held in the Free Church on occasion of Dr. Burroughs's temporary removal to Marseilles. Pastor Humbert stated that, in an assembly which crowded the building, "two hundred and fifty persons, of all ages, rose up as one man to declare that they had found Christ in our evangelistic meetings." Mr. H—— designated it as "the most memorable hour in thirty-five years of ministry." We understand that eighty of these persons had entered into membership of that Church.

LORIENT, BRITANNY.

Payment for Converts.

M. Kissel, the zealous young pastor who directs our work here, writing in 1883, details the singular but ineffectual methods resorted to for deterring the people from coming to the meetings. He states that it was gravely announced in leading circles of the town that the secret of so large an attendance had at length been discovered. "For the conversion of a man (*i.e.*, inducing him to declare himself Protestant), we pay 700 francs (£28); for that of a woman, 400 francs (£16); for a child, 100 francs (£4); or for a year's attendance, once a week, without conversion, 40 francs." M. Kissel adds that not a few gravely credit this grotesque report. The work in dark Britanny has gone onward with evident blessing. There are now two stations at Lorient amidst the seafaring population, and he longs to open a third, if funds allow, in the centre of the town. The missionary ship visited it this year, and sometimes as many as a thousand persons pressed to the spot, desiring to attend the services.

Ajaccio, Corsica.

Ajaccio, the chief town of Corsica, is, like most things in this world, far more attractive when seen from afar than when one is in it. The new quarters, however. are clean and airy, and the city is decidedly civilised. It is beautifully situated on a splendid bay, with lofty mountains in the background. The bay is shut in, as it were, by a group of small islands, which look romantic when the sun sets upon them, but which bear an ugly name : *Les Iles Sanguinaires* (The Bloody Islands). As the passenger sees them and hears the name on entering the bay, he has a fair representation of Corsica : physical beauty and moral destitution.

Ajaccio is the birthplace of Napoleon. The house of his father and mother is still in the possession of his family, a large, unpretending structure, in one of the narrow streets. One of the Bonaparte princesses still lives on the second floor, while the first, the old apartment of Madame Lœtitia, is shown to visitors. The plain, heavy-looking furniture is still there ; not a thing has been changed since more than a century. The whole world was turned upside down by the conqueror, but his cradle has remained in the same state since his birth. Here is the bed on which he came into the world ; here is the little desk on which, as a boy, he used to write his school-tasks.

Alas ! Bonaparte has done very little for his native islands. What a man of the sword can do to remedy moral misery, even when he has a desire to do it, is very little indeed. No land in Europe, I suppose, is in a sadder state morally than Corsica. The Gospel, even the Roman Catholic Gospel of the Middle Ages, never thoroughly penetrated the country. The native savagery has been, as it were, varnished with a tint of Christian civilisation, which some of the many invaders of that unhappy land brought with them. But there never was a true missionary in Corsica; no Columba, no Patrick, no Augustine, ever went there. In the southern parts, the Mussulman occupation has left traces in the manners as well as in the features of the people.

Corsica has no religion. It is externally Roman Catholic, but without the fanaticism which reigns, for instance, in Sicily. They believe in a God, and, like all rural and primitive races, they are religiously disposed. But they have only two dogmas : the worship of Napoleon and the *vendetta.* Their moral sense is very low indeed. And yet their intelligence is remarkable ; they are fond of knowing, they read and travel more than the average Frenchman. In the interior, far away in the mountains, it would be difficult to find a man who cannot read. They are hospitable, and very much attached to those who give them cause for gratitude.

We have been led to establish there a Mission, which was not, however, the only attempt of the same kind. But no Society had been able to persevere long enough to make an impression. A London committee was formed a few years ago, through the initiative of a great friend of Corsica, Mr. Cecil Berger, to evangelise the interior of the island. A few months afterwards, we began a similar work in the cities : Bastia and Ajaccio. Through lack of funds, the first of these stations has been given up, and we have now only one foothold in Corsica : Ajaccio.

Our missionary there, M. Mabboux, seems providentially fitted for the place. He is strong and persevering, courageous and full of faith. He loves the Corsicans, a requisite quality which very few Christians possess. He, his wife, their mother and their sister, have all been converted in the Mission in Paris, and they are all at work, each according to his or her ability.

Our *salle* has been removed into the very heart of the city (17,000 inhabitants), and M. Mabboux reports, twice a week, an attendance of about one hundred and fifty, mostly men, the women being difficult to reach. Some time ago, when, through our sore financial distress, we had been obliged to consider whether we must not give up even that station also, we received a letter, signed by sixty men, begging us not to send away a man who was so useful, those signing considering themselves as members of a new community of which he was the pastor.

We should, however, say that these do not by any means represent as many real conversions. The minds, the sympathies, the friendship of a good many have been gained; but the change of heart, the new birth required in order to make such a change solid and secure, has not happened in every case, perhaps only in a very few as yet. But our missionary is full of hope, and would not, he says, exchange his field for any other.

He does not content himself with the work in the city. He has preaching stations all round in remote villages; for Corsica is scantily populated (260,000 inhabitants for an island which is twice the size of a French department with 350,000), and the villages are far from each other. His letters are full of interest, showing the difficulties and even dangers of such evangelisation, for in many places the priests are fierce against him, and do all they can to hinder him. Where the priest has no popularity (as is frequently the case) the opposition of the clerical man is a help rather than a drawback; but when, as it also happens, the priest belongs to a local family, and has many relatives, cousins, and friends, the clannish spirit takes hold of them, and the evangelist might be in danger were it not for the spirit of grace and prudence that God has given him. In no case, however, would fanaticism cause serious opposition, except on the part of the women.

We commend our evangelist, his family and work, to the earnest prayers of God's people. The Corsicans are born soldiers and sailors ; a more daring, more courageous race could not be found. If Christianity should take hold of them, they would make, with their great intelligence, splendid missionaries.

In Bastia, about ten converted Corsicans remain, the fruit of our labours. One of them is a young man, who has had to suffer much from his family on account of his faith. We have no doubt the Lord Himself will be their Pastor, and notwithstanding their ignorance and isolation, will keep them safe, and make them a blessing to others.

R. Saillens.

P.S.—Ajaccio is a growing winter resort. There is comfortable hotel accommodation, an English Episcopal church and chaplain. The country, the climate, are beautiful. The new quarters of the city are pleasant. The distance from Marseilles is fifteen hours in first-class steamers (twice a week). Why should not some of our friends try and go there for a season ?

The Soldiers' Reading-room, Marseilles.

If a visitor enters the hall, 59, Boulevard National, Marseilles, between five and eight on any evening of the week, he will be startled by an unusual sight. A hundred soldiers, or thereabout, in their blue jackets and red trousers, are seated quietly on the two sides of half a dozen long tables, filled with books, writing-paper, and ink-bottles. On the walls, under the texts taken out of the Word of peace, hangs a formidable panoply of swords, with red *képis* above them. The contrast between this military display, these striking colours, and the peaceful attitude of the poor fellows makes a great impression. Here is one, his two fists under his jaws, deeply plunged in the reading of a good book ; another, beside him, gently inclines his head over his shoulder, and

smiles complacently at his achievements, his tongue hanging
between his teeth : he has been putting the last flourish to
the signature of a letter, laboriously penned, which he is
going to send home.   Meanwhile, in a corner of the room,
a group of six or seven is gathered round Mademoiselle
Stahlecker, our devoted missionary, taking a lesson out of
the Bible.

It is particularly at Christmas that the *salle* is full, and
the writing home a most important affair.   Mademoiselle
Stahlecker at one of these seasons wrote :—

" I write you on pretty rose-paper, to give you a sample
of our soldiers' letters to their parents for New Year's Day.
They are all busy writing home, and I am thus kept in the
salle, during the last days of the year, up to eleven o'clock
at night.   I have also a few sergeants, who prepare themselves for St. Maixent (a military school), and who bring me
every night a composition to correct for them. . . . I am
surprised to see how meekly those big *moustaches* accept
the little sermons I preach to them."

In another letter she says :—

" Our numbers have risen this year to 17,250 attendants,
i.e., 4,000 more than last year.   We often have had as many
as two hundred at a time in the hall, especially in the last
days of the year."

It has been the privilege of the writer to speak more than
once to these dear fellows ; for it is a principle with Mademoiselle Stahlecker to invite frequently some preacher of the
Gospel to come and speak to them.   I do not think one could
find a more sympathetic audience.   They frequently applaud
the simple preaching of the Gospel ; and they are fond of
the hymns.   Mademoiselle Stahlecker keeps up a correspondence with several who have left Marseilles, their time
of service being over, and who are thankful for what has
been done for them and taught them.

When one realises how many and how dreadful are the

snares which Satan puts before these young men, and how important it is for this country that the new generation should be influenced by Christian truth, one cannot but thank God that He has so manifestly qualified our dear sister Mademoiselle Stahlecker for such a mission. May He continue and increase His blessing upon the worker and her difficult field !   R. S.

We have now similar soldiers' reading-rooms in a number of our stations.

The Missionary Boat ("Bateau Missionnaire").

For several years past, in summer, Mr. Henry Cook, of the Portsmouth Seamen's Society, has placed one or other of the missionary boats at our disposal and that of other Christian workers in France. This (to the French) novel method of evangelisation has been attended with most evident marks of Divine approval.* The campaign of 1886, embracing many before unvisited places in dark Britanny, reads like a new chapter in the Acts of the Apostles. The following quaint and characteristic fragment is from the pen of our devoted missionary M. Etienne Sagnol, describing the visit to Boulogne-sur-Mer in August, 1883 :—

"The outside of the *Annie* has nothing unlike other vessels. But we were not a little surprised with the perfect accommodation inside, and the adaptation of every corner and available space : beautiful inscriptions on the walls, rows of shelves, cupboards and drawers full of Bibles, tracts, hymn-books, in various languages, a little harmonium, and forms with backs, to the great comfort of the people.

"We began our meeting at Boulogne-sur-Mer with a good attendance. Pastor Dégremont presided. We noticed with pleasure the *serieux* of the people, and the hearty way they sang. All who have visited Boulogne have been in-

---

* Many thousands of French seamen and others have thus been brought within the sound of the Gospel for the first time in their lives.

terested in the *matelotes*, or fish-women, with their peculiar
dress made of brown-reddish linen, and their white bonnet,
whose fore-part is in the shape of a fan, making their
faces look as though surrounded by a nimbus. Some of
those came to our meeting. Let me tell you of one. I
had been to one of the public fountains, erected on the
quay, to get refreshed between two meetings. There stood,
with her two pails, a rather old *matelote*, with her nimbus,
like a saint in a church picture. When she saw me beginning my toilette, 'Wash yourself in my pail,' she said.
'Thank you much,' said I; 'and won't you come to our
boat to hear about Jesus?' 'Oh, Jesus! I know Him
well,' she said, 'and perhaps more than you do. Do I
love Him? see my chaplet; I have it always with me, and
every year I go to the convent yonder for a month in order
to pray and make penitence : more so, I have been several
times in pilgrimage, and lately to Nice.' 'Well,' said I,
'the rather you should come, because we also pray to Jesus,
and love Him much.' 'All right; but I have no time to
go, because I rise early in the morning, and my eyes pain
me at night with the lamp-light.' 'But you'll stay only a
little while if you choose, for I should like very much to
see you there.' I had finished refreshing myself; she saw
me looking for my handkerchief, so, turning her back, she
said, 'Take my apron; there is a clean corner somewhere
behind.' Said I, 'Oh, you are too good,' feeling rather
dismayed at the proposal, for I felt very suspicious about
finding a cleaning spot on her working attire; but seeing
my hesitation, she speedily undid the tape round her waist,
and I was obliged to obey her gesture, not to miss my
opportunity of winning her. She looked very pleased at
me, saying, 'You are not too proud with the poor people.
I am very glad to do an act of humanity to some one well-
dressed.' I had finished drying my hands, and was taking
leave of her. She said, 'Make a little prayer for me, won't

you?' 'This I will do,' said I. 'Good-bye, sir.' Half
an hour after, as the people were coming for the meeting,
what was my joy to see my obliging friend coming and
asking me to show her a seat! The meeting began, and we
spoke of the finished work on the Cross, of the blood that
cleanseth, of the freeness of access to the Master of earth
and heaven, to whom it was better to apply than to anybody
else, because He said Himself, 'Come unto ME.' I noticed
my good woman with eyes sparkling with joy at the good
news of free pardon, and immediate assurance of salvation.
One after the other we spoke, adding *témoignage* to
témoignage of the glorious truth. Blessed be the Lord,
I saw her crying, with others. The meeting went on, but
she did not move before the end, when she came to me on
her way out, saying, 'Thank you, sir; I am confounded
with joy to have come. I'll come with my people to the
boat here.'

"Notice was given that a meeting for the soldiers would
take place every day at six o'clock. We had a very good
audience of our *pantalons rouges*. I have never seen a
more attentive audience than these soldiers. Mrs. Robert-
son, of the Society for the Free Distribution of the Scriptures,
enabled us to give each soldier a copy of the New Testament. They came in increasing numbers up to the last
meeting.

"Among the crowd attracted by our singing were numbers
of children. We could not allow these to come on board,
for want of space. It tore our hearts to be obliged to keep
these little ones at a distance, so we thought we might have
a meeting for them alone; consequently we told the people
in the boat and the children outside that we should be
pleased to see them at four in the afternoon, one of the
boys wanting the meeting at four in the morning! They
came long before the time, and we had the privilege of
talking to these dear little ones, who were so very good

that I would give them as an example to any trained Sunday-school anywhere. We taught them hymns, verses of the Bible, selected so as to instruct them in the simple truths of the free grace for those who repent and look to Christ for forgiveness. Miss Blundell, who has given kind help during the last week of our sojourn in Boulogne, has at every meeting won many a young heart by her touching stories. I thought good to ask the children if they wanted me to think of them when in Paris. 'Yes, yes, sir!' 'Then give me your names, all those who want me to remember them.' This was no little work for the writers to take the names of all those willing, for nearly two hundred children gave not only their names, but also their addresses.

"On Sunday was our last meeting. The people seemed as if they would not go away. In the after-meeting M. Dumas said, 'If you believe that what we have said is true, and are determined to live accordingly, lift up your hands, that we may rejoice in knowing it, and pray for you.' We saw a hundred hands raised, and a hundred faces radiant with joy. We spoke with English, German, Swedish, and Norwegian sailors. We have given to them Gospels and tracts. We have sung with them, we in our tongue, they in theirs. We trust that though the work, by the kindness of the Lord, was great, still greater results will follow the Word of God we have left with these people. A new meeting has also been held once a week since we left, in a room secured very near where the *Annie* lay."

III

"*GIVEN WITH THANKS.*"

AMERICA'S CONTRIBUTORS AND CONTRIBUTIONS.

BY THE REV. W. W. NEWELL, JUNIOR.

THE Rev. Dr. Goodell, of St. Louis, invited me into his pulpit to tell to his people the story of the McAll Mission in France. After the service he said to me, " My dear brother, our offering for France is *given with thanks ;* remember, it is GIVEN WITH THANKS."

As I went out into the brilliant sunshine of that winter Sabbath, the 31st of January, 1886, aglow with the inspiration of that superb congregation and of their princely gift, these last words of their noble pastor rang a deeper joy in my heart : " *Given with thanks ; remember*, GIVEN WITH THANKS." Alas ! there was little possibility that I should ever forget. These were the last words of Dr. Goodell to me. That night this valiant leader was suddenly promoted to the heavenly ranks. And on the morrow, as the whole city wept their loss, these words came to me as a fitting motto of a noble life : " *Given with thanks.*"

To-day, called to review America's contributors and contributions, the thought of the grateful generosity of the Church of the New World recalls this motto and gives title to this chapter. Whatever sacrifice America has made, whatever offering she has sent for the advancement of the McAll Mission, all has been given with thanks.

If this chapter recount the interest especially of America in behalf of our Mission, it is because Mr. McAll requests it. He himself has written of the valued effort of his own land. And yet I beg here to bear testimony to the consecration and generosity I have often witnessed in Great Britain, and which, from the first days of this Mission, have fed its life and growth. The Christian world will never forget that it was an English pastor, with his devoted English wife, whom the Lord called to the inception and development of this work, a work which is far more than the McAll Mission in France, which has given birth and type and even name to blessed Christian work in other lands. And the Church will always love Christian England the more dearly for the name McAll, as she does for Whitefield and Bunyan, and hosts of others.

America does not forget that it was that grand Scotchman the Rev. Horatius Bonar, D.D., who first told us that the fields of France were white unto harvest. This book was a glad revelation to the Church of America. So eagerly was it read that a New York publisher put it into cheap form as one of a popular library, and the inspiration of that book is still sending forth labourers into the harvest.

But before this, fugitive efforts had been made in America in behalf of the McAll Mission. It is gratifying to find in our first annual report the names of two Americans who had visited the Mission in its cradle, and contributed to its support.* And thus

* Dr. Agnew and Morris K. Jessup, Esq., of New York.

from the first existed that *international co-operation* which has been such a significant feature of our Mission.

From time to time those acquainted with the work in France have visited the American Churches and told what they have known. Prominent among these have been Miss Beach, M. Réveilland, the Rev. Mr. Dodds, the Rev. Dr. Beard, M. Saillens, the Rev. Robert McAll (cousin of the founder of the Mission), the Rev. Mr. Greig, Mrs. Le Gay, the Rev. Mr. Berger, and the Rev. Mr. Bracq.

Mr. Moody, the American evangelist, while in Paris became deeply interested in the McAll Mission, and has since borne kindly testimony to its efficacy. At a meeting of business-men of Chicago last winter, called by Mr. Moody in the interest of mission work in that city, he said, " I consider the McAll Mission the model Mission of the world. I cannot tell you how deeply I was impressed by the sacrifice of Mr. and Mrs. McAll, giving themselves so completely, and without salary. It is the best-run Mission I know. That is just what we need here in Chicago, and in every large city of America, a mission not of churches, nor of chapels, but of shops or stores right on the busy thoroughfares where the people are, many of these open every night of the year, with a band of devoted workers, men and women, who go from station to station, thus giving a needed variety, and who have but the single aim to win lost souls to Christ."

Miss Elisabeth R. Beach.

The campaign of Miss Beach was so unique in its character and so telling in its result that it demands more than passing notice. Miss Beach was the daughter of a New England clergyman. Gifted with an attractive person, a joyous disposition, a mind of more than ordinary talent trained by a broad education, and a deep, all-pervading Christian character, Miss Beach was a lady of peculiar charm and culture. Coming to Paris for the study of the French language, she found introduction into a circle of refinement and learning. Among others, the venerated Rosseeuw Saint-Hilaire, Professor of the Sorbonne, delighted to converse with her, gave her cordial welcome to his home, and came to look upon her as a member of his own family. From Professor Saint-Hilaire Miss Beach learned about the McAll Mission, and she soon caught the enthusiasm of this noble Christian for the growing work.

At that time the Rev. E. W. Hitchcock, D.D., was pastor of the American Chapel in Paris. He and his little flock assumed the support of two of our mission-rooms, and sought to supply the working force of these stations. He secured the co-operation of Miss Beach, leading her to work in the *salle* at Les Ternes. This work became with her a passion, and she counted these hours in the Mission as the happiest of her life in Paris.

Nor had she neglected her studies. On her return to America she was at once invited to the professorship of the French language in one of the leading lady colleges of the United States. This position offered to her an honourable reward for her industry and a wide sphere for intellectual and spiritual influence.

Meanwhile, she could not forget the McAll Mission. In her visits after the home-coming she told of Mr. and Mrs. McAll and of their work. Her friends were delighted with her story. Among others, she met the Rev. Dr. Chamberlain. He was so deeply impressed

THE LATE MISS ELISABETH R. BEACH.

that he urged upon her to repeat the story to the ladies of his congregation. Miss Beach was frail and timid, the very opposite of what is called "strong-minded." She was sure that she could not utter a word at a gathering even of ladies. But at length Dr. Chamberlain prevailed. The service was so effective, that Dr. Chamberlain asked her to repeat it in a neighbouring city. All the delicacy of her nature shrank from this. But the gentle firmness of Dr. Chamberlain, the forced acknowledgment that to speak to her sisters in Christ of the work of Christ was far from indelicate, and the conviction laid upon her conscience of the precious result of such a service for the loved Mission, all these persuaded her consent. She went from city to city, from State to State. All that winter of 1880 she was pressing on her glad pilgrimage. The result was immense. The many thousands of dollars gathered were a precious boon to the Mission. But what is more, Miss Beach grouped these ladies together as auxiliaries, laid upon them the responsibilities of the work, and pledged them to permanent effort. Nobly have these pledges been redeemed. All these years the Mission has been nourished by the increasing offerings of these auxiliaries.

Pastors of wide experience in methods of Christian work and of awakening to missionary endeavour have said, " We have never known a more effective campaign than that of Miss Beach." And her honoured friend Professor Saint-Hilaire has written to Mr. McAll : " From this journey of our devoted sister Miss Beach, which God blessed beyond all that could be foreseen, dates a new era of sacred brotherhood between the Christians of America and those of France."

One of the most delightful instances of the permanent influence for the Mission started by Miss Beach is the devotion of the Rev. A. F. Beard, D.D. From Miss Beach Dr. Beard first received definite knowledge of the McAll Mission. It was largely due to the interest thus awakened that Dr. Beard afterward consented to direct in America the telling journey of M. Réveilland and the Rev. Mr. Dodds in behalf of the general work of French evangelisation. The next step, he was led to become pastor of the American Chapel in Paris; thus he became a director of the McAll Mission and one of its most valued friends and helpers.

It is fitting here to mention the aid rendered to our work by the American Episcopal Church in Paris. The Rev. Dr. Morgan and his people were in the midst of building a very expensive church edifice, the finest American church building in Europe. And yet, burdened as they were with the labour and the expense of this construction, they expressed their growing interest in our Mission in assuming the whole expense of one of our important stations in Paris, and as far as possible aiding in its working.

But to return to Miss Beach. Alas! she had gone quite beyond her strength. For years she suffered from pain and weakness. Then came a touching incident. Those whom she had enlisted in behalf of the McAll Mission were now her most helpful friends. Lavishly, tenderly, lovingly, they cared for her. She was welcomed to their homes, provided with the best of nurses and physicians, sent on long, expensive journeys by land and by sea, and all by those who yesterday were strangers, but who to-day loved her and cared for her for Christ's sake.

How blessed and blessing are these ties in Christ. Miss Beach said to me one day, " I am not worthy of this expense of money and effort. It ought rather to be doing some positive work for Christ." I could but answer, " My dear friend, you fail to see that your illness has its Divine mission. Not only are many cheered by your gladness in suffering, but God is using your feebleness to develop the most Christlike of graces." This thought comforted her. She slowly responded to this loving care. All her dream for this world was to return to the work of the McAll Mission. There was increasing probability of this happy result. In the spring of 1884, to avoid the cold winds of New England, she was sent by these same loving friends to the South. She was very hopeful that this might be her last journey before her longed-for voyage to France. Alas ! in a few hours the steamer, the *City of Columbus*, was wrecked, and her frail body was washed ashore by the wild waves of the merciless tempest. It was a sudden home-call. But long time she had awaited this as the happiest call which could invite her.

And the brave, priceless effort she had made for the Mission—did she regret it ? The last message she ever sent to Mr. McAll was full of hope for recovery and return to Paris. "But," she added, "if my effort for your Mission shall yet cost me my life, as possibly it may, I would not recall it. The importance of the work is more than worthy any sacrifice I could make." Thus, as a fitting epitaph of her grateful consecration, may be written, " *Given with thanks.*"

As a memorial these friends in America now support a special station of our Mission in Paris. It bears her name—"Salle Beach." It is situated at Les Ternes, near the Arc de Triomphe, within a few steps of the room where she once engaged in her loved work, and where she is still teaching many the Gospel of Christ.

American McAll Association.

But there is a yet more notable monument to her zeal. By numerous visits and innumerable letters the Rev. Dr. Chamberlain aided in keeping alive the interest of these auxiliaries. Several of these ladies discovered a rare executive ability, quickened by an absorbing consecration to this work.

No. 1,622, Locust Street, Philadelphia, is a fine double city house, the home of the venerated Isaac Lea, LL.D.,* presided over by his accomplished daughter, Miss Frances Lea. By happy providence, Mrs. Marine J. Chase is an inmate of this home, an acknowledged and beloved member of the family. To this home, remarked for its refined taste and royal hospitality, celebrated as a rendezvous of men of literature and science—to this elegant home Miss Beach found introduction and hearty welcome. It was a happy moment for the McAll Mission when this frail girl stepped over that threshold. From that visit this noble mansion has become the *American home* of the McAll Mission. And to aid our work Mrs. Chase, Miss Lea, and even grand old Dr. Lea himself, devote their wealth, their influence, their strength, themselves. What incalculable blessing this has wrought! In many cities there were friends of our Mission devoted, disinterested, capable. There was need of those who should give themselves wholly to it. There was need of a central point about which

* See note on Dr. Lea's death, p. 88.

these interests could be grouped. There was need of
those who should not only guard the interests of our
Mission in their own Church or city, but who should
also develop this interest in cities altogether unin-
terested. This is exactly what God found for us in
this home. Here was born the idea of a National
Association for the mutual quickening of these auxiliaries
which remained, and for a positive, organised effort to
multiply these auxiliaries throughout the United States.

On the 29th of March, 1883, representatives from
three auxiliaries—from Philadelphia, Brooklyn, and
Washington—met together at Philadelphia and organised the American McAll Association. Soon afterwards Mrs. Chase was naturally chosen president,
and Miss Lea treasurer. A vice-president was chosen
from each State in which an auxiliary existed, among
the most prominent of these Mrs. President Garfield,
of Ohio. The Rev. Martin Luther Berger was chosen
representative secretary. After careful study of the
work in France, he returned to go literally from city
to city organising auxiliaries, turning back from time to
time to revisit those which were formed, and stir them
up to new life by new intelligence of the work. The
Rev. J. C. Bracq now performs this service. And a
wonderful success these beloved brethren have scored.
At the third anniversary of the American McAll
Association (April, 1886), they chronicled *thirty-five*
auxiliaries, with promise of continued increase. As this
goes to print (November, 1886), they number *forty-nine.*
Wise, untiring efforts have been made to provide these
auxiliaries with information of the work. Unnumbered
letters have been written. For Mrs. Chase alone the
correspondence has been so immense that one spring

her hand was nearly paralysed with writer's cramp. A racy *Quarterly Record* is published, containing the latest news of the Mission and tidings of the auxiliaries. Well-known French and American writers are asked to write articles, which are published as leaflets, tracts, or pamphlets, and scattered broadcast. These have great weight and charm. Need was felt of a literary secretary or editress. And here again the American McAll Association has been signally provided for. Mrs. Louise Seymour Houghton, whose writings have been so eagerly read, and who for years rendered valuable service in the work of the Mission in Paris, has graciously accepted the direction of this department.

Spontaneity.

From this sketch several characteristics of the interest in America may be noticed. Perhaps the most striking feature is that this has been *spontaneous*. It was not the McAll Mission which sent Miss Beach to America to seek aid for our work. The conception and consummation of that priceless effort was entirely in America. We only received the results. The American McAll Association was not organised by the directors of the Mission. They never dreamed of such an event. They were simply notified of its existence. Every step forward has been suggested in America and accomplished there. While for some beloved Societies it is difficult to awaken and perpetuate the needed and deserved interest for their work, for the McAll Mission America, unasked, has given herself.

And this we accept as a precious token of the Divine favour. In France there has never been human scheming to open doors for the advance of the Mission. God has opened the way before us more rapidly than we could follow. Thus also the Lord has gone before our effort in America. Funds have come to us which were all unsolicited; and friends have offered themselves whom we had never seen, of whom till then we had never heard.

Interdenominational.

Another happy feature of this effort in America, as also of the work in France, is that it unites various Church denominations in harmonious co-operation. It has gladdened many a Christian to find that in the McAll Mission, Congregationalist, Episcopalian, Presbyterian, Methodist, Baptist, Lutheran, and others work side by side in Christian unity. Here is therefore one mission for whose support all denominations can unite. This has delightfully obtained in America, and often clergymen and laymen have said, " While ·we thank God for His blessing upon this work in France, we also rejoice for its blessing to us, in bringing us closer together and offering to us a platform where we can work together in the fact and spirit of Christian union."

Organisation.

It is significant also that our friends in America have *organised* for the purpose of moving America in our behalf. While complicated machinery is often cumbersome and clogs itself, yet a simple organisation is often essential to large and enlarging endeavour. It is as true in religious as in other affairs that what is every one's business is no one's business. The American McAll Association is simple enough to be elastic in its workings, and yet organic enough to work. The Christian ladies of a city are called together to decide whether or no they will form an auxiliary of the McAll Mission. A favourable decision being arrived at, necessary officers are elected, among these a vice-president from each evangelical denomination, and as far as possible two or more managers from each evangelical Church. The auxiliary thus formed is associated with the National Society. Thus it receives constant information of the work in France, and various literature bearing upon the work. The auxiliary is also visited from time to time by the representative secretary, or by friends from other auxiliaries. Meetings of the auxiliary are held at stated times, when papers are read by some of their own number, or addresses delivered by a pastor or layman who may possibly have visited the Mission in France.

Variety.

If it be seen that many ways are adopted for keeping alive and developing the interest of an auxiliary, it is also true that there is fullest liberty as to the methods of raising money. Generally managers seek subscriptions by calling upon members of the Church they represent, or a collection is secured from the Church, or a Sabbath-school gives of its Mission fund, or a Sabbath-school class makes a special offering. Sometimes it is *only a letter.* A gentleman of Morristown received a letter telling of the needs of one of the workers in France. This gentleman had extracts from the letter printed, called a meeting of the members of the evangelical Churches, and so put the matter before this meeting that the whole sum of *seven hundred*

6

dollars was assured from this little village. And they have given more than this amount every year since. *The young ladies* devise various methods of securing aid—a tea, a concert, or a sale. Sometimes a circle of young ladies is organised which combines the study of the French language, literature, and history with a careful study of the Mission, and thus is secured a broad familiarity with the work. Often interesting papers have been prepared to be read to the auxiliary to which the circle belongs, adding to the general information and interest.

In the city of Washington the summer heat drives away all who are not forced to remain. In the winter, during the sessions of Congress, the social and religious life makes serious demands upon one's time. Several young ladies wished to do what they could, yet knew that it would be a mistake to attempt too much. They resolved that they could meet together week by week during two months in the autumn and two months in the spring—four months of the year. They therefore call themselves "Le Cercle des Quatre Mois." And really valuable work they have accomplished. Besides the intellectual and spiritual enjoyment, they secure a large part of the salary of one of the best Bible-women in France.

In several instances a McAll auxiliary has been formed in young ladies' seminaries or colleges, and with blessed result.

This culture of a missionary spirit among the young must tell for good. A clergyman of marked prominence said to me, "The McAll Mission is doing much for us in America. It prompts the interest and effort of a large number of young ladies who have heretofore shown little sympathy with mission work ; and the experience they are now getting in behalf of your Mission, above all the spirit of consecration thus awakened, promise much for the future missionary activity of our Church."

A very interesting incident has lately come to our knowledge. A lady felt that the *boys* had been over-looked. She invited a few lads to her home, told them something of the McAll Mission, and asked them if they were ready to band themselves together to aid this work. They gave a hearty approval, and, with the promptitude of boys, set to work to see what they could do. It is interesting to note the various ways in which they saved or earned the money. They held meetings from time to time, and studied up missionary work in general and the McAll Mission in particular. Those few boys were able to send more than *one hundred and twenty-five dollars in six months.* Writing of this happy result, this Christian lady drops the hint that there are many boys of many cities who would gladly follow this example were they but invited.

Consecration.

As has been already seen, God's children are moved by His Spirit to a consecration to our Mission which in many cases amounts to sacrifice. The result has been large ; but let it not be imagined that this accrues only from large gifts. Many a poor widow in her little chamber has sought from God the means to spare yet one more mite. Many a poor child has given its only *sou* that France might hear the Gospel.

Sorrow has also sent its sacred offering. For a fuller share in the Lord's work seems a fitting association with our loved ones who share the Lord's glory, and the winning of souls to Christ seems a fitting memorial of those who dwell with Christ. Often in taking, the Lord rebukes our withholding.

Two brothers, Scotchmen, engaged together in business, suffered heavy losses, and were threatened with speedy failure. They came together before the Lord to ask why they were thus afflicted. The conviction came to each of them, "We have not given enough to the Lord, and have thus proved ourselves unworthy of larger trust." They then solemnly promised God that if He should see well to prosper them in business, they would give a fixed and large share into His treasury. From that day they had such success that they became immensely rich ; and nobly they have kept their pledge. Their superb beneficence has blessed innumerable good works, and to-day the surviving brother is one of the largest contributors to the McAll Mission. Are there not others who are tending to poverty through withholding ?

Responsibility.

The last characteristic of the American endeavour for the Mission which shall be mentioned, is a widespread sense of *personal responsibility.* Not only Miss Beach, Mrs. Chase, and Miss Lea—many others share their compelling consecration. One lady asked her pastor how she could move the Christian influence of their city in behalf of the McAll Mission. This city had never been visited by a McAll worker. This lady had but slight acquaintance with our work. The Lord seemed to have laid upon her this responsibility. Her pastor replied, " You must give yourself to this effort. You must think the McAll Mission, and talk the McAll Mission. You must eat the McAll Mission, and drink the McAll Mission. You must take it to bed with you, and you must arise but to follow it." She did, and the eloquence of her earnestness moved that city. A thriving auxiliary was formed where many had declared this impossible, and to-day she lives with the same consecration for the life and growth of the auxiliary to which she gave birth.

A remarkable determination that the interest of their auxiliary shall not wane is displayed by some of these ladies. The calls in America are innumerable, not only because of the large responsibilities to the missions of foreign lands, but also because of the unprecedented responsibilities at home. That the privileges of the Gospel may keep pace with the march of population and civilisation over our immense territory demands enormous outlay. The response is generous, but the pressure is intense. One interest crowds out another. It often demands a zealous wisdom to keep alive one such interest year after year. The president of one of these auxiliaries found last winter that there threatened to be a sad falling off in their receipts. At once she made this a personal matter. After prayerfully looking at the question, she invited to her home the officers and managers of this auxiliary. They came in large numbers. After a pleasant tea, she said to them, " Ladies, you all know that our offerings this year for the McAll Mission have been very small. We must do something. But I confess I have nothing to propose to you. Each one of us must accept her personal responsibility before God in this matter." Very little was said, but this president felt that these ladies came

together feeling that it could not be done, and went
away *resolved that it must be done.* The next monthly
meeting was ten days after. As Church after Church
was called, each representative came forward, giving
to the treasurer an envelope marked with the sum it
contained. When the roll had been called, and the
amount added up, the treasurer arose and with
trembling voice announced the result—*more than seventeen hundred dollars* (£340) *in ten days.* Tears dimmed
many an eye as they simultaneously arose and sang,
" Praise God, from whom all blessings flow." Thus
did they declare their generous effort " given with
thanks." Nor was this all. At their next monthly
meeting these ladies brought *one thousand dollars more.*
And this had been impossible had they not felt themselves personally responsible to accomplish it. They
will be surprised enough to find their effort in print ;
but such recitals have their mission. There are multitudes of God's children in many lands who long to do
more for Christ, and who eagerly accept every sugges-
tion as to increased possibilities of work. It is not so
much to bear deserved testimony to the consecration
and success of our friends over the sea that this
chapter is written, but to encourage to new endeavour
those who are asking, " And what more can I do ? "
It is not so much a history, as a hint to girls and boys,
to women and men, that to willing hearts there is many
a way to accomplish more for the Master.

And let no one imagine that this is only in the interest
of the McAll Mission, but rather for the culture of a
missionary spirit. How various God's calls to-day !
As never before, not only France, but the world, waits
to receive the Gospel. Not one Christian is exempt.

Isaac Lea L. L. D.

Possibility means responsibility. And never was there
such generous giving of means and of self, never such
noble army of ready ones who accept all, achieve all,
with gladness and gratitude.   And thus we are brought
once more to the title of our chapter, which shall be
voiced this time not in America, but in England.   With
Mr. McAll, I once attended a drawing-room meeting, in
behalf of our Mission, in the elegant home of a well-
known London banker.   After we had told the story of
the Mission, this Christian philanthropist arose and said,
" What a blessing it is to us that God makes use of our
money for such a work as this ! It is because our
Lord's servants have need of us that they come and
tell us these glad tidings, and give to us the inesti-
mable privilege of sharing with them in these sacred
endeavours."   Beloved Christian friends throughout the
world, such consecration at home makes missionary
work easy abroad.   Your glad zeal and loving faith
quicken us to new attaining.   And whether we give our
offering and ourselves *for* the work or *in* the work, we
sanctify all with the same glad spirit : " *It is given with
thanks.*"

WILLIAM W. NEWELL, JUN.

NOTE.—See p. 77. After the writing of this chapter, before the
correction of the proof, we have received a cablegram announcing
the sad news of the death at Philadelphia of our venerated friend
Isaac Lea, LL.D., at the advanced age of ninety-four. We deeply
mourn our loss, and extend our heartfelt sympathy to the large circle
of afflicted friends.

EXPERIENCES OF A FRENCH EVANGELIST,
1871 TO 1886.

BY THE REV. RUBEN SAILLENS.

I.

O N Christmas Day, 1873, the writer was on a visit to his parents, settled in Paris. He was then a student of the East London Institute, founded by the Rev. H. Grattan Guinness, and had come to spend the Christmas vacation in Paris, partly with the view of acquainting himself with a new and strange mode of evangelisation, which had been lately commenced in the capital of France. And so it happened that on the afternoon of that day, at five o'clock, he entered for the first time one of the halls of the McAll Mission, then in its infancy.

He had never before spoken in public to his own countrymen, his only experience as a preacher having been made on the waste places of the Mile End Road in the east of London. Previously, it is true, he had worked in, and indeed had started, the Ragged Schools of Lyons, which had so well succeeded that as many as seven hundred pupils attended those schools at the end of the previous year (1872). But speaking to a set of rough children in a provincial city was quite another

thing from addressing an audience of grown-up people in
the metropolis of France.   For Paris is, in the mind of a
provincial Frenchman, the city wonderful and terrible,
which at once attracts and repels him.   Everything
good or bad comes from thence; no revolution suc-
ceeds, no movement of any kind, which did not originate
there.   The people of such a city must, of course, be
a special people, witty, full of criticism, ready to
detect any defect in the poor fellow who presumes to
come and teach them anything.   Such were the impressions of the young evangelist on that day; no
wonder that he rose with fear and trembling when
Mr. McAll, with a smile, asked him to speak !

On what text should he preach ?   There were a few
words printed on a bill which was largely distributed
at the door: "English and French friends wish to
speak to you on THE LOVE OF JESUS CHRIST."   This
would be his subject; and he soon forgot the strange
audience, and everything besides, in the blessed endeavour to make plain to these working men of
Ménilmontant, who were far, poor fellows! from being
acute critics and sneering infidels, the wondrous love
of Him who came to seek and to save that which
was lost.

Such was the first connection of the writer with this
work, his first meeting with the man who was to be
his leader for many years to come,—years which, he
trusts, are far from their term,—the Rev. Mr. McAll.
At that time, this English name was not familiar to
the young man, and, indeed, was not much known in
France.   There were even in Paris Church members
and pastors who knew nothing, or scarcely anything,
of the great work which had begun at Belleville about

eighteen months before. How was it that at once the heart of the young student was linked to this new enterprise and to its founder? It would be impossible to say, except that it was God's doing. The Lord had led His youthful servant in strange paths; from a secular business he had been moved to give himself to Missions; then, a great obstacle being in the way, he had decided to become a regular minister. A visit of Mr. Guinness to Lyons had changed his plans, and he had gone to London to prepare himself in order to become an evangelist. And now, before his training was over, Mr. McAll made a pressing invitation to him to settle in Paris and become his regular helper.

The invitation was accepted, and six or seven months later, the young man left London altogether, not without carrying away a blessed remembrance of his intercourse with such distinguished Christians as Mr. and Mrs. Grattan Guinness. It was fitting that an apprenticeship to the evangelisation of the masses of Paris should be made under the care of the above-named friends, who, even before Mr. McAll had come to Paris, had themselves preached the Gospel in that city, helping Pastor Armand Delille to start those meetings of the Rue Royale which ever since—throughout the war, the siege, and the Commune—have been carried on with much blessing.

II.

At the time of his definite settlement in Paris (August, 1874), the young evangelist found the Mission still in its infancy. Not more than five or six halls, most of which were smaller than the present average size, had been opened. The installation was of the simplest

kind ; a plain calico sign was stretched on the door-
way, with the big letters, "Aux ouvriers! Réunions
gratuites." A kind of lantern, also in calico, was hanging over the door, with a lamp inside, and the same
words reproduced on the panels. No gas, but a
number of clean petroleum lamps, lighted the interior.
The walls were merely whitewashed, with a few texts
or illustrations nailed upon them.

These were the heroic times of the Mission. Few
people then seemed to believe in it ; nobody, even its
own founder, would have prophesied the wonderful
increase it would take by-and-bye. The staff consisted
of Mr. and Mrs. McAll, M. and Madame Rouilly,
and a few English ladies. As the writer looks back
upon these youthful years, they appear to him under
a mist of poetry. How sanguine, optimist, hopeful, he
felt as, every month or two, a new hall was being
opened, and new crowds heard the Gospel !

The members of the Mission lived on the same spot,
on the heights of Belleville. There was the main
station, a beautiful hall crowded every Sunday night
with three to four hundred hearers. From that quarter,
the workers went and came back together to and from
the other halls established in the distant parts of Paris.
Oh, those long rides in the small and slow omnibuses !
It took them an hour and a half to go to Grenelle, then
a small and unpromising station, which has now become
one of the best of the Parisian *salles*.

In this first period of the Mission's history, the
meetings had a more intimate, more familiar, and more
informal character than they have taken since the en-
largement of the halls and the accession of many new
speakers. The ladies—Mrs. McAll, Madame Rouilly,

Miss Wilkinson—had no objection to take part in them
by reading a piece of some good book or periodical.
Then Mr. McAll would follow with one of his addresses,
which he read, not a sermon, but a simple tale illustrating the power and the blessedness of the Gospel
of Christ. The hymn-book consisted of two or three
sheets, and most of the hymns had been written by
Mr. McAll himself, the airs having been chosen in some
English hymnal, with much taste, by Mrs. McAll.
Those hymns showed in their author a strange, a
remarkable knowledge of the French rules of prosody,
and a still more wonderful power of the will. " We
want hymns, we have none, we *must* have some ; " and
he had set to work. Some of them will remain in the
French hymnology ; their intrinsic value, apart from
the name of their author, will make them, I have no
doubt, precious to future generations of worshippers.

This, indeed, was missionary life. Mr. McAll could
be found in the morning writing an address or a
hymn, and in the afternoon in some remote quarter
of Paris, looking out for shops to let, or in some new
hall about to be opened, nailing texts upon the walls
and setting the chairs in order. Meanwhile, the young
ladies rested from their labours of the previous night's
meeting by pasting, covering, and mending the hymn-
books or the periodicals which were given to the
public to read every evening before the meeting commenced. Yes, there was a great deal of drudgery work
which the evangelists had in that time to do themselves, and which, as the Mission has grown, it has
been found more expedient to leave to other hands.
But these labours in common, this oneness of purpose,
created among the small staff, isolated from all society

A.F. Beard, D.D. E. Réveillaud. R. Saillens. R W. McAll. Mrs. McAll. W. W. Newell, jun. C. E. Greig.
Mrs. Legay. Mrs. Newell. Miss Johnstone. L. Sautter.

but their own selves, a friendship and an intimacy which seldom exists to such a degree in organisations of the same kind.

III.

As his pen runs over the paper, the writer sees before him many a dear face now absent from the congregations on earth, but present in those above. Belleville especially was the field of his labours. There had the Mission begun, and there was the largest of the halls. The sight of that Sunday night congregation was enough to make any Christian man eloquent. Here, in the midst of that quarter which, two years before, had witnessed the savage scenes of the Commune, ten minutes from the spot where the Archbishop of Paris had been shot, was an old dancing-hall full of poor people dressed in their best clothes, and listening intensely to the good news that God had not cursed them for any deeds of theirs or of their fellow-men.

Among those hearers were an old gentleman and his wife, *petits rentiers*, as the phrase goes, who lived in a secluded part of the quarter, and never missed a meeting. The old man was something of a scholar, a bookworm; he had taken a liking to the young preacher, and undertook to help him in his classics, alas! sadly neglected. So he lent him literary books, and in exchange the young man lent him religious ones. The *rentier* and his wife were Catholics, of that old type of Catholicism which did not altogether exclude a shadow of good sense and liberalism; their faithfulness to the meetings, their reverence for the Gospel, the sobriety of their lives, were truly edifying. However, it took them long to understand the golden

principle of the Gospel of Christ: salvation by grace. But
the old man, before dying, showed that he had both comprehended and apprehended that all-important doctrine.

In another station, there was a dear old lady, always
cleanly attired, with a white bonnet round her nice
old face, such as grandmothers wear in our remote
villages. She, too, had taken a liking for the young
missionary. She was not talkative, and could not be
easily approached, but she was a diligent and intelligent
hearer. Once she came up to the preacher after the
meeting, and asked a call from him. " I will go," said
he, and he went on the next day. Her room was as
tidy as herself, though she was poor, and had to work
for her support. " Well," she said, " you have come !
I want to give you something for what you have
given me. Here are fifty francs [and she took them
from her small treasury in the wardrobe]; please
accept them ; don't refuse me." There was no
alternative but to accept the money, which she consented to be used for mission purposes.

His visits in the lanes and courts of Ménilmontant
and La Villette unfolded to the young soldier of the
Cross mysteries of sin and woe he had never dreamed
of, for his knowledge of East London life had been
small, owing to the difficulty of the language. But
here he had to listen to stories such as are never found
in books : women whose husbands had fought under
the Commune, and had been sent for years of penal
servitude to New Caledonia, poor creatures left alone
with children to care for ; working men without em-
ployment ; households without bread ; demoralisation,
sin, misery, misery everywhere !

There were also cheering occasions. Sometimes the

young man would come into a house just when the
Bible was being read. A long conversation would
ensue, neighbours would be called in, and thus a little
meeting held in a garret. This happened more than
once. Truly the people of the Paris faubourgs, notwithstanding its then recent dramatic history, seemed
at that time nearer the kingdom of God than any other
population. It has not ceased, I believe, to be so ; only
hitherto *the means of making known the Gospel have not
been equal to the needs*. At that period there was little
done outside the McAll Mission, which was then supported almost solely by English contributors. Honour
and love to these dear English Christians ! One of
them, George Moore, was the first to bring to famished
Paris a morsel of bread ; and another, Mr. McAll, was
the first to bring us the bread of life ! Whatever
diplomatists may do, we shall never cease to love our
English brethren.

On the track of past recollections, it is difficult to
know where to stop. I should like to speak of La
Villette, where Miss Wilkinson and I had to contend
with a Sunday-school that was too numerous for us,
followed with a meeting that was too small. In the
former we had eighty rough fellows all to ourselves,
while at the adults' meeting only six or seven people
deigned to gratify us by their presence ! And oh ! how
the young preacher felt down-hearted one Sunday
afternoon, when, after a more powerful sermon than he
ever had preached, the only man in the audience who
seemed to have been impressed told him, " Well, now,
I am pleased with you. You must be thirsty. Come
and have a glass with me." The offer was well-meant,
but of course respectfully declined.

7

Meanwhile, the Mission was growing. Ten or twelve stations had been established, and new workers, several giving their voluntary services, others more or less supported by the work, had been added to the staff. In 1878, the McAll Mission and its workers took a prominent part in the special efforts put forth at the great Exhibition. In common with the Evangelical Alliance, Mr. McAll erected a pretty hall near the Trocadéro, with accommodation for five or six hundred people. Two meetings were daily held in it, with great success, sometimes the place being quite full. A large distribution of tracts and Gospels was made at the doors, through the liberality of the English Bible and Tract Societies. This campaign was one of great fatigue, but also of great encouragement. Here we had listeners from all parts of France, people who, in their own country, would never have gone to hear a Protestant preacher. The results have not all been known, and yet we have heard of persons who afterwards declared themselves on the Lord's side, and who had received there their first saving impressions, not only residents in Paris, but also visitors from the provinces, from Spain, and even from South America.

IV.

Two years before this (1876) the writer of this sketch had been compelled, in common with all his fellow-countrymen of the same age, to serve in the army. The minimum duration of service—twelve months—he had to pass in the large and busy city of Marseilles, a city well known to him, for he had spent in it his infancy.

Near the barracks was established a small reading-room, founded by those devoted friends of the French soldiers Mr. and Mrs. George Pearse. Every Sunday night a little meeting was held in that place, to which the working men of the neighbourhood were invited. The young Christian soldier attended those meetings, and sometimes spoke in them. He was struck with the eagerness of the people to come, for the reading-room was in a very unlikely street, and there was a narrow staircase to climb; but notwithstanding these drawbacks, as many as a hundred people, civilians or *militaires*, would crowd the room. This gave him the first idea of carrying the McAll Mission, which hitherto had kept within the walls of Paris, to the provincial cities also.

It would not be, perhaps, interesting to the reader, and would make this paper too long, to tell how it came to pass that, at the end of the Paris Exhibition, 1878, the writer and his young family left the capital in order to start in Marseilles a similar work to that of Mr. McAll. The Rev. Mr. Dodds, whose untimely death all the friends of the Mission have lamented, had just arrived in Paris, and Mr. McAll had found in him a devoted, efficient, zealous helper. The writer more and more had come to feel it was his duty to do something for the rest of France. God had providentially put in his way those that would help him in the first steps. One of those parties was the committee of the Young Men's Christian Association of France, and the other a generous English Christian, the friend of many missions, W. T. Berger, Esq., of Cannes.

The first mission-hall in Marseilles was opened October 28th, 1878, in that same district where the barracks were situated, a densely populated quarter. This was the first attempt of the kind ever made in

the Phocean city, which hitherto had the reputation
of being bigoted and shut to all Protestant influence.
Yet as many as the *salle* could hold came to the meetings ;
indeed, the influx was such, that, after a few weeks,
it was found necessary to enlarge the room, and to
make it large enough to receive three hundred and fifty
people.   Through God's grace, the means came in
abundantly, and it was possible, three months after the
evangelist's arrival, to open a second hall at the other
end of the city, in the quarter of Mempenti.   Here the
success was for some time unparalleled in the history
of the Mission.   A vast concert-hall was filled twice a
week with as many as seven hundred and fifty people,
not a motley crowd gathered out of mere curiosity, but
a regular set of hearers, quiet, and hearty, and sympathetic.   The Sunday-school numbered four hundred
pupils.   It was a grand time.   The converts of the first
mission-hall helped in the work of the second one.
They came in a large band, about forty of them, men,
women, and children, and went back to their own
quarter when the meeting was over, singing hymns on
the way.   A good number were added to the Churches ;
many, though they did not join a Protestant congregation, became nevertheless true Christians.   There was
a whole house, with its first, second, and third floor,
where all the *ménages* belonged to the Mission, the
husband or the wife, or both, having been converted in
it.   Those good people held meetings in each other's
apartments.   There was among us a genuine, though
quiet, revival.   Much of the success was due to the
earnest, disinterested efforts of the pastors of Marseilles,
foremost among whom was my friend Pastor Creisseil,
who gave much of his time and strength to the Mission.

Cool-headed people will say that it was a mistake at this juncture to extend the work instead of deepening that which was begun. Perhaps it was so; but it could hardly be expected that a young missionary, with hundreds of thousands of living souls around him, would not undertake as much as he possibly could do, and perhaps a little more. A third hall was opened in the Rue de la République, then a fourth, then a fifth, and the Mission came to have nine stations in the large city of Marseilles.

Although the excitement of the first days had gone, the work proved genuine, for a large number of these converts have stood the test of years, and are now among the faithful members of the Churches.

Not long after his own beginning in Marseilles, the missionary was called upon to help in the beginning of similar missions in various towns, especially in Annonay, Valence, and Nice. The work in this latter city, one of the most difficult to evangelise, on account of the deep demoralisation and profound ignorance of the native population, had been undertaken by a local committee, and managed by a student of theology, now a distinguished Free Church pastor, M. Louis Guibal. But when the student had to leave Nice in order to return to his studies, an appeal was made to Marseilles to take the management of the work; and then it was that the Nice Mission became a branch of the Marseilles one.

V.

At a general meeting of the southern branch of the Young Men's Christian Association, there was a young man, aged twenty, with dark features and a deep musical voice, who made a great impression on the writer. His name was Sully Clavel; he was an orphan, and had not received a proper education. He had never left his own village, where he earned his living by cultivating the fields, and even sometimes breaking stones on the public road. But that young man had a great piety, coupled with a wonderful intelligence. By a kind of intuition, he had learned to preach the Gospel in chosen terms, and with real eloquence. Apart from the gifts of the Spirit which he possessed in no ordinary measure, he had also wonderful gifts which seemed to mark him out as a leader of men.

"Will you leave your stone-breaking and come with me to Marseilles?" was the question put to Sully Clavel. He asked time for consideration and prayer, and finally answered, "Yes."

When the people of the great city heard him, they soon fell in love with him. He was gentle and affectionate—but so ignorant! In order to fit him for service, it was essential he should be taught. Lessons were arranged for him, and thus it was that the School of Evangelisation of Marseilles was founded.

Another helper became necessary, and was found also in an unlikely quarter. A young Christian was serving his time as a soldier in the little town of Aix, not far from Marseilles. On Sundays he would come over and attend the meetings. He also had already preached the Gospel previous to his enlistment, and now he could be heard, at Mempenti or La Belle de Mai, in his soldier's attire, giving testimony to the power of God to keep a man happy everywhere, even in barracks. That young man was M. Chaigne, now our successful agent in Toulouse. He accepted the call of the Marseilles missionary to become his helper at the end of his term of service ; and thus three young men had all to themselves the evangelisation of the queen city of the south.

It would be tedious for the reader to find here a detailed account of the progress of the work, thus entrusted by the Lord to inexperienced hands. He made it manifest, notwithstanding many shortcomings and lack of faith, that His blessing was on it. He heard the prayers of His children ; when money was wanting He always sent the amount required, some-times just at the point which verged upon distress. Praise be to Him who takes up the smallest among the children of men, so that it may be evident that to Him, and not to them, belongeth the power !

Another accession to the little staff was very im-portant. It was that of a Christian lady from Alsace, Mademoiselle Stahlecker, whose previous history is interesting, as showing the marvellous way in which the Lord trains His children for a special work. The dear Christian who had hitherto managed the little reading-room for soldiers mentioned previously had to retire, on account of her great age. Mademoiselle Stahlecker undertook this branch of the work. The library was transferred to our hall of La Belle de Mai, and a great blessing has attended ever since the endeavours of Mademoiselle Stahlecker. For years the reading-room has been daily attended by military men, sometimes more than a hundred sitting around the tables, and seldom less than sixty. They read good books; they sing hymns ; they hear the Gospel. Several have been converted. Mademoiselle Stahlecker has a large correspondence coming from those who, after having returned to their country, have not forgotten the *salle*, and wish to continue in the path in which they have learned to walk.

Several other young men had been added to the School of Evangelisation. The devoted pastors of Marseilles had, with much competence, turned themselves into professors, and the evening meetings offered a beautiful practising ground for the students. In fact, the grand principle on which that school (now under the management of Pastor Richard, and independent of the McAll Mission) was established was that all the young men being trained should have engaged in Christian work before coming, and should work while studying. There never were more than seven at a time ; several are now engaged in missionary work at home and abroad.

Another branch was added to the Mission of Marseilles.

Not far from the Continent, half-way between Europe and Africa, in the Mediterranean Sea, stands that island of Corsica of which Rousseau prophesied that some day " it would astonish the world." It has done so, indeed, in a manner that he could not have foreseen. The journey from Marseilles is short, and there is almost daily communication with that island.

An English gentleman, Mr. Cecil Berger, had been struck by the needs of Corsica, as we had been ourselves, and he had decided to make an effort to have the Gospel carried to the peasants of the Corsican mountains. He asked the Marseilles missionary to become his agent, and to accompany thither an evangelist he was about to send. The request was cheerfully as-sented to, and thus it was that the writer made his first journey to the neglected island. It was a most interesting tour. Everywhere the people greeted the missionaries, and were eager to hear them and to receive their books. There was just enough opposition to create an excitement which helped the work rather than otherwise. After this first journey, two evangelists were sent: one supported by the committee of which Mr. Cecil Berger had taken the initiative, and another by the Marseilles Mission. The latter was understood to work especially in the city of Bastia, while the other enterprise had for its scope the villages and the mountains.

The work in Corsica has continued ever since 1881, and has been extended to the capital of the island, Ajaccio. As yet little visible fruit has come of it. No land has been so saturated with human blood as this land; no population has been so sadly neglected. The Corsican race is a mixture of the Visigoth, Lombard, and Moorish invaders of the land, with the Celtic population which occupied it in remote times. Never was a true apostle sent to these people. Christianity was imposed on them by the Italian republics which ruled them, but it was never preached by a true missionary, like Augustine, or Patrick, or Columba. This explains why the Catholicism of that island is far inferior in type to that of any other Roman Catholic population; in fact, *Corsicans are still heathens* in their manners and customs, especially in the awful practice of the *vendetta*, still so popular among them. While there is a strong religious tendency, there is no particular attachment, on the part of the men, to the Church of Rome. Corsica offers, we believe, a unique field of labour in the world, and it is with great sadness that, owing to the depression of our funds, we contemplate the probable necessity of passing over to other hands the evangelisation of that land.

But we must pass over many interesting details. Another branch was started in Cannes, at the request of a few friends there. All these stations—Nice, Cannes, Corsica—were provided with evangelists by the Marseilles school. A great trial and a great loss fell on us. Sully Clavel, that remarkable preacher of the Gospel, so full of promise and so popular among the *habitués* of our stations, was taken away from us, at the age of twenty-five. His end was peace. Though engaged to be married, and full of plans for the future, he was enabled to lay all aside, and to say, "Thy will be done." The writer will ever consider the fact that Sully Clavel died under his roof, and that he was a witness of his triumph in death, as a great privilege. Five hundred of the regular hearers of the departed preacher attended his funeral, covering his coffin with rosettes of flowers and crowns of pearls. A tomb was erected to him by subscription among them. Oh that God would raise, out of the Huguenot Churches, a few scores of such young men! The reformation of France would soon be accomplished.

VI.

A trial of the same kind came on the Paris Mission in September, 1882. We need not say much upon this, as all the friends of the McAll Mission know the details of this terrible event. The Rev. Theophilus Dodds, a young man of thirty-two, father of five children, and the right arm of Mr. McAll in the management of his growing work, was suddenly cut off, poisoned by a dish of toadstools, which had been taken for wholesome mushrooms.

This blow went to the heart of the writer. Though independent of the McAll Mission, he had not ceased to consider himself as a son of it, his apprenticeship having been made in it. A personal tie of sympathy united him to Mr. and Mrs. McAll, and had never been broken. The oneness of purpose of the two missions seemed to make it desirable that they should be one in all things. This had been hinted previously, both by Mr. McAll and by other friends, but the necessity of such a union never imposed itself so much on the mind of the writer as at this trying juncture. After considering the matter before God, he resolved to accept the proposition that had been made to him, and the Marseilles Mission was joined to the general one.

This involved the writer's return to Paris. The opinion of many friends, which he had to accept, was that, in the lack of men of which the Mission suffered, his place was in the main city of France, his special gift being not so much to manage a detailed organisation, as to preach the Gospel as often, and to as many, as possible. In Marseilles, much time and strength was lost in the necessary cares which fell on the missionary alone, the result being that his preaching was hampered. All these considerations, but above all the need which Mr. McAll seemed to have of a younger man to fill somehow the place made vacant, led the writer to the decision which has been mentioned above.

Since July, 1883, the date of his return to Paris, the young evangelist has often looked back with something like regret on his own field of Marseilles. Notwithstanding the fact that the work there was entrusted to good and able hands, it has come to a standstill, and it could hardly be otherwise. But he has been comforted by the hope—he could venture to say the assurance—that his labours in Paris have compensated whatever might otherwise have been done in the south. A mission to America enabled him to make a thorough acquaintance with that wonderful country, and to stir up there the sympathies for France which had previously been awakened by the departed Miss Beach, and by Messrs. Réveilland and Dodds. This increased sympathy has enabled the Mission to open larger halls than ever before in quarters that hitherto had never been touched. The evangelist is thus able every week to preach the Gospel to twice as many people as he could have met with in the ordinary times of the Marseilles Mission. This seems to him a sufficient reason for the removal of his labours to Paris, however painful it is to see the southern branch, through lack of funds and other causes, suffer and decline somewhat from its former importance.

And now he has been led to settle in the very midst of that large city, so as to be able to reach by personal intercourse those who have been impressed in the meetings of Boulevard Bonne Nouvelle, his special station, and of the Rue Royale. Interesting cases spring up almost every week. There is room, in that central part of Paris, for one of the largest churches in the world, and there is the possibility of it. For nearly two years and a half, winter and summer, a congregation of three hundred has been seen at Boulevard Bonne Nouvelle *every night,* and another of the same size, at ten minutes' walk from the former, on Boulevard

INTERIOR OF THE SALLE, BOULEVARD BONNE NOUVELLE, ON A SUNDAY EVENING.

de Sébastopol; six hundred faithful hearers thus gather
daily; and if the halls were doubled, no doubt, sometimes at least, the congregations would be doubled also.
Out of this large number of sympathetic listeners, how
many have believed? We venture to say, Hundreds
since the beginning of the work in these quarters.
But where are they? Some in the Churches, but
many out of them. This is the question we have now
to meet, if we wish our Mission to produce large, permanent, and traceable results, and a lasting movement
among the French people. An effort of some kind,
as broad as may be wished, must be put forth to form
those people into a Christian Society. They want it,
they ask it; may God give us the wisdom, the courage,
and the necessary grace for the solution of this difficult
but most urgent problem!

In conclusion, the writer would say, though he has
not attained the age of the ancient prophet, " Hitherto
hath the Lord helped us." Unworthy of the blessings
received, he yet dares to crave for more. And he
humbly commends himself and his beloved country,
which is passing now through the greatest moral crisis
of her history, to the prayers of those who love the
Lord and wish to hasten His promised epiphany.

R. SAILLENS.

V.

THE WORK AMONG THE YOUNG.

BY THE REV. CHARLES E. GREIG, M.A.,

Superintendent of the Juvenile Department of the McAll Mission.

TO understand the opportunities and the methods of this section of the McAll Mission, the best thing is to see the field and the work with one's own eyes. I therefore avail myself of two papers written indeed some years ago, but never published, which will do more than pages of disquisition to explain to our readers the efforts we are making. The Roman Catholic Church has long recognised the importance of laying hold of the young, and has astutely availed itself of the influence so gained; but Protestant Missions, with some noticeable exceptions, have strangely directed their main efforts to calling adult sinners to repentance, and have looked upon the training of the young as a very secondary aim. How we try to reach them, and how far they respond to our overtures, these papers on the schools of the Faubourg St. Antoine and Montreuil will show.

But what is the Faubourg St. Antoine? It is only a long, not very wide street, with a row of tall houses on each side, houses often eight or nine stories high, with old black oak staircases inside, and long narrow entry courts running back from the main street, not too clean for the most part, and known nearly all over the world as one of the most lawless parts of Paris. For in the great French revolution at the end of last century, it was from those same tall dingy houses of the Faubourg St. Antoine that the half-starved, thinly-clothed men swarmed out to pull down the great fortress of the Bastille, which shut out the western sun at one end of the street; and it was again from the same houses some months later on that a band of gaunt ragged women set forth impatiently, determined to force their way into the presence of the King, and demand " bread and an end to all this nonsense." That is what the fathers and mothers of the Faubourg St. Antoine were capable of a hundred years ago, and it is not much more than ten years since their great-grandchildren did very much the same thing, or even worse, so it cannot be said to be a very quiet, respectable locality. All the more reason why God should put it into the heart of Mr. McAll to open a mission-room in this riotous quarter, where the Gospel of peace could be proclaimed to this turbulent community; and already the street is quieter and less revolutionary. Let us take the top of a tramway from the Place de la Bastille, where the tall iron column of Liberty now replaces the old prison, and have a look at this redoubtable faubourg.

At first one sees a constant succession of furniture shops, dark and narrow most of them, but extending far back from the street, and full of beautiful furniture; then come smaller shops, eating-houses—"To the Negro," "To my Aunt," "To Puss-in-boots," etc., greengrocers, tool depôts, vendors of low prints and penny dreadfuls; then, after passing a large hospital, with trees in front of it—Hôpital Trousseau, or Ste Eugénie, the children's hospital of Paris—one begins to notice old women standing in the doorways, or sometimes just at the edge of the pavement, trying to sell vegetables, fruit, herrings, cheese, boot-laces, cheap trimmings—everything, in fact; suddenly you come upon a large fine shop occupying a whole block, a *magasin de nouveautés*, having just opposite it a particularly narrow dirty cross-street, always full of ragged children, playing and squabbling in the gutter; but this great effort at respectability seems to exhaust all remaining possibilities, and though the street gets broader, the houses get drearier and more deserted-looking, till at last we come out upon a wide open space with a fountain in the middle, and guarded at the far end by two tall pillars, from the top of which gigantic figures of kings look tranquilly out into the country, turning their backs upon noisy Paris; and we perceive that we are in the Place de la Nation, and have left the mile-and-a-quarter-long Faubourg St. Antoine behind us.

But the mission-room? We never saw it! No wonder, for it is a very quiet affair! Three doors higher than the *magasin de nouveautés*, on the same side of the street, is a court, at whose entrance a man with black goggles sells thread, tape, buttons, and such things; and looking past his stall, one sees at the end of the court a glass door, with "Salle de Conférences" printed on it. That's the place. Suppose we go there in company with the superintendent some Sunday afternoon, what shall we see?

It is five p.m., and very dark and cold, for this is a winter school we are going to visit, that in summer differing slightly, chiefly in respect to numbers. Though quite as cold as in England, perhaps almost colder, so biting is the wind, the street is much less dark, owing to the large number of shops still open, especially restaurants and cheap jewellers'. When we reach the *magasin de nouveautés* before mentioned, we begin to notice a row of children standing up against the wall, trying to fancy they are warm while they wait to be let in, while swarms of others are playing "hide-and-seek" or "soldiers" across the street, regardless of the numerous trams, carts, and carriages. As soon as they catch sight of the superintendent, there is a shout raised of " There he is ! " and they pitch themselves upon us to shake hands and to ask to be let in, for though they have never seen us before, it is a sufficient recommendation that we are the friends of their friend, and we are adopted on the spot. We struggle on, say, " Good-afternoon," to the button-man at the entrance of the court, and straightway get lost in a sea of children, who are crammed up tight to the door of the hall. More hand-shaking, and inquiries after the father of this one, and the mother of that, and the little brother of another, and the hand of a fourth that was crushed in a machine, and so on, and so on ; while we are astonished to see that though they are so numerous and so wild-looking, nobody is pinching his neighbour, or pulling somebody's hair, or otherwise making mischief ; they are all quite good, though very noisy. At last we get to the glass door, open it, and find ourselves in what seems to be a large room, with one little gas jet burning about the middle of it. There is no difficulty in shutting the door, though the children are all clamouring to get in : " Not yet," says the superintendent, and they stop pushing.

But our hands have already been seized by some quiet sort of people, whom we can scarcely make out in the darkness, and when more gas has been turned on we find ourselves surrounded by some fifteen or sixteen teachers, mostly young and all alert-looking. The room is large and not uncheerful-looking now that the numerous jets are all lit, but as compared with an American Sunday-school, and even with some more recently built ones in England, it is bare in the extreme. On the whitewashed walls are seven or eight large texts, made by pasting letters cut out of silver paper on turkey-red cloth ; a plain deal platform occupies the middle of one side, on which are a harmonium, a table, an *armoire*, and one or two chairs : on the *armoire*, propped

up against the wall, is a large blackboard. That is abso-
lutely all the furniture, except about three hundred straw-
bottomed chairs, arranged in convergent rows facing the
platform ; nor can I say too much, on closer inspection, for
the cleanness and salubrity of the place, yet not many halls
in Paris are looked upon by their *habitués* with more pride
and affection than this. But while we have been looking
round, the superintendent has been greeting his teachers, and
putting things in order for the opening. It is no fault of his
that he is not the first to arrive, for this school is only the
third he has conducted to-day, and several of his helpers can
say the same. It is no holiday task, evangelising in Paris,
and these men and women do not look as though they made
light of the combat ; almost all converts of the Mission,
we are told afterwards, and the eagerness visible on every
face, though mixed with so many other expressions, had
already made us suspect it. It is no desire to follow the
fashion that has brought them here, nor any routine conception of Christian duty ; " life " is written all over them, even
in the attitudes they assume in the various little groups. A
description of one or two will show what sort of material
Mr. McAll has at his hand for regenerating France. Look
at that little woman talking eagerly to a tall grave girl ; her
face is all drawn to one side by a blow received in childhood,
but her eyes are bright and laughing, and she seems just
overflowing with animation. In at least five different parts
of Paris you could find scores of children who could tell you
her name, for to her professional duties of Bible-woman she
adds a most unquenchable enthusiasm for the little ones. Born
of nominally Catholic, though really indifferent, parents, she
very early became anxious about her soul, and for many
years sought to work out her own salvation in observing to
the letter all the requirements of the Church of Rome ; but
four years ago she wandered into one of Miss de Broen's
meetings, and there heard for the first time that her sins

were forgiven her for Christ's sake. One or two conversations with the Belleville evangelist, M. Van der Beken, convinced her of the truth of the marvellous news, and her natural earnestness soon showed itself so unmistakably in the field of Christian effort, that she was asked to accept a permanent post. Childless herself, her pent-up mother-love showers itself upon the big girls who gather to her class, and whom she can warn from her own knowledge against the dangers of work-room and sales-room life. Nearer the door is an oldish man, with a long grizzled beard and a slight stoop; his face seems to have very much the texture, as it has the colour, of an old shoe, but his eyes are deep sunk beneath shaggy eyebrows, and piercing; in his hand he carries a stout walking-stick, and on his shoulders is hung a curious hairy cloak. He is talking, or rather discoursing, with a great deal of gesture, to an active little fellow with a black moustache. He is a colporteur, known all round about Paris for his pertinacity and extraordinary tact in dealing with scoffers of all kinds; he is a Protestant born, but does not hesitate to declare how little worth his Protestantism was till he found his way to the mission-halls. Each face seems deserving of study. Yonder is a man who might stand any day for a soldier of the great Roman republic, so completely does he recall the indomitable proud endurance of those free citizens; near him an American art student, learning rapidly to model with equal skill the soft clay and pliant child-nature. But let me point out rather one of the ladies, one of that devoted English-speaking band who do so much to help forward our work. She is erect and tall, much the tallest of the lady-teachers, and looking more so from the ulster which covers her from neck to heels, and which seems to suit that energetic, whole-souled nature which not so many years ago used to drive distracted her worthy Sunday-school teacher in Scotland, and make her almost despair of ever even taming the wild impetuous girl. But God touched her heart, and though she is not at all clever, and had almost to be forced to take a class, her influence over the big bad boys in it is unbounded. Take a good look at her as she stands there with her hands in her pockets, giving tit for tat to a curious lithe-looking lad who balances himself on the back of a chair in front of her, the very incarnation of a Parisian *gamin*, for if the McAll work in general owes much of its success to that spirit of devotion which its agents have caught up from its founder, the work among the children owes even more to those noble ladies who have worked on in the midst of much discouragement, clearing the ground, filling up gaps, making the gentleness of the Gospel felt in the wildest gatherings, and then quietly disappearing, or contenting themselves with a subordinate place, when the fully qualified superintendent came on the field.

But all this time we have been leaving the children surging at the door, and now the clock opposite the platform marks 5.13, and the teachers gather together for a short prayer before the door is opened. And then what a rush ensues! Every now and then the superintendent has to bar the door with his arm to give time for those who are already in to settle down in their places before others push them up behind, and the dozen teachers have quite enough to do in guiding them to where they should go. Let us introduce a few of them, to show the sort of children among whom we work. One of the first to come in will be a bright-faced boy named Henri David, who a little time ago gave so much trouble to his parents that they sent a message to the superintendent asking him to speak seriously to the lad, for he was on the high-road to prison. He has now much improved, comes most regularly, and his superfluous energies can be utilised in keeping the others in order. Not far behind him will be his sister, older than he, and strongly built, with a calm intelligent

face. She carries a little boy in her arms, and a small girl
is beside her, for though she is only fifteen, her decision of
character has already made her the queen among the
children of the district.   It was well for us that the Spirit
of God laid hold of her young heart, for her influence now
is wholly on the side of good and of order.   Not far off is
a taller, very pretty girl of the same age, but much more
slightly built and less decided-looking.   These two are
great friends, and only a year ago they were so ill-behaved
in the school, talking and exciting the others, that they had
to be spoken to seriously.   They said nothing at the time,
but came up some minutes after to their teacher and asked
his forgiveness, promising that he would never have to
speak to them in that way again.   Nor has he.   The
prettier of the two was some time after told by her mother
that if she persisted in going to that silly school, she must
do so in her working-dress, and rather than miss the Bible-
lesson that girl took her seat beside her gaily dressed
companions in her old apron and faded skirt.   But here
rushes up quite a little boy, very ragged, but open-faced,
and snatches off his dirty cap before putting his hand into
his friend's, while his sister, less ingenuous, slinks in behind
him.   These are little street-singers, or rather they were,
for their mission friends have just succeeded in getting
them put to school, but they have still all the winning
graceful ways characteristic of their profession.   Their
father and mother have each a wooden leg (one is often
inclined to wonder that the children's are both of flesh and
bone), and gain very little money.   Still they are honest,
and try hard to train up their children respectably.   Much
sadder is the lot of another boy, who comes tumbling in
head over heels, his unbrushed hair and ragged blouse
betokening a "nobody's bairn."   He is known in the street
where he lives (one of the worst in Paris) as *little Louis*, for
he has neither father nor mother, and lives "anyhow."

But under the ragged blouse beats a warm heart. From the door, where he has just given the superintendent a frank shake of the hand, he makes one dart across the room to the tall lady in the ulster, and rustles up into the warm cloth with a look of entire confidence. When she visits in his street, he and his friends, who are never too pressed with work, form her bodyguard, and escort her safely from house to house, and then homewards along the faubourg. But how can one go over them all? The little boy whose gumboil burst, says his sister triumphantly, just after his teacher had left the room after praying that the little man's pain might be relieved ; the girl who slipped on the stair as she was bringing up a jug of milk and hurt her knee so badly that she still walks lame: " But I didn't spill a drop ! " she shouts eagerly, as her mother tells the story,—these and many more are not only known to the great Father of all, but well known to us too, so much individuality of character is there among the voluntary adherents of our schools, the children who come because they want to come, because they feel they must come, because their own tenacity of purpose triumphs over all obstacles put in their way.

Once the three or four hundred in the hall, the school goes on much as any other would. After prayers and singing, an address is given, bearing more or less on the lesson of the previous Sunday, at the close of which permission is given to the more restless spirits to retire at once, if they wish. The remainder then break up into classes, to study for half an hour the international lesson, till the bell calls them all together again. Then comes the most distinctive feature of the whole day's work, the questioning of the whole school from the desk with the help of the blackboard. the object being partly to impress the truth more firmly on the children's mind partly to show the teachers how they should have taught

Then, after a short prayer, the classes go out one by one, any child who wishes to speak to the superintendent returning after the general dispersion, and coming up in turn to him, as he sits prominently behind his black table.

Nor should we forget the tea to which the teachers sit down together about seven. There is hardly one of them who is not looking forward to some service in connection with the evening meetings in the different halls throughout Paris, and the prosaic necessity of physical sustenance first suggested this common meal, but it has been maintained and even imitated elsewhere for much higher reasons, as tending to knit together the workers in a way that no formal meeting could accomplish.

But this school has been in existence for years, and is thoroughly organised. What about one that has been newly opened, or where the staff is insufficient? Let our second paper answer that question by showing

How the Children started the Meeting.

Every visitor to Paris knows the great cemetery of Père La Chaise, but probably not many have cared to inquire what there is beyond it. Let us suppose that some tourist, more enterprising than his fellows, bestirs himself soon after dawn on Sunday morning, and wends his way past the Bastille column into the densely populated Faubourg St. Antoine. Here his attention might well be arrested by certain large two-horse conveyances of the omnibus description which he sees frequently passing him in one direction or the other, marked all of them " Montreuil." Curious to know what this Montreuil may be, which seems to keep up such a lively traffic with Paris, let us suppose that our tourist resolves to follow one of the aforesaid vehicles. About half-way down the faubourg he observes that it branches off up a narrower street, called, like itself, "of Montreuil," and feeling sure that he is on the right track, he allows the coach to get out of sight. This Rue de Montreuil, as before said, is narrow, dirty also, and much crowded with hawkers and travelling merchants of all descriptions. In time it is seen to cross in quick succession three large boulevards, all radiating from a large column-adorned place, which our friend's guide-book teaches him to call " of the Nation," jealous Republicanism having so changed the former "du Trône." A line of tramway has now added its more convenient means of transport to the red coach, and the street has widened out a little and dashed the hair back from its face, so to speak, though still dirty and out-at-elbows. Next, the Ceinture railway is crossed, hastily, under the watchful eye of beuniformed officials, and at last the fortifications are reached. " C'est la porte de Montreuil," a green-coated *douanier* politely informs our tourist. To his surprise, no sooner has he stepped beyond the walls than a rather pretty landscape opens out before him. In front, it is true, is a somewhat squalid-looking village, but to the right is a pleasant vista of tree-surrounded villas, dominated by the double donjon of the old fort of Vincennes; while on the left is an extensive stretch of market-gardens, ending, on the Paris side, in a fort-crowned grassy slope, and farther round, in the abrupt eminence the Parisians call a *butte*, clothed from head to foot with vineyards, and surmounted by a thick, well-planted wood. But though our tourist recognises all this with pleased eye, his attention is immediately arrested by a most extraordinary rag-fair just at his feet. Here are piles of old hats, in every stage of decay, artistically arranged one on the top of the other; there a fair assortment of coats, not of the latest fashion, showing signs also unmistakably of a green old age; a little farther on, an immense collection of rusty tools, broken locks, unmanageable keys, and anything else that can come under the head of old iron; a little to the side, three open umbrellas arranged like portions of a great spider's web, at whose centre sits the merchant, an old lady of no pretensions to beauty, holding a fourth umbrella over her head, probably to preserve her complexion. Beside her a donkey examines contemplatively a mixed assortment of crockery, and resolves, apparently with some contempt, that the whole lot is not worth a kick of his hoof, an opinion not shared in by a vagrant urchin, whose destructive projects are blighted by an unexpected demonstration in the rear, obliging him to beat a hasty but not over-silent retreat. Farther back, several ragged boys are attempting to fly a kite, while their sisters roll about in the dust, squabbling over some wretched stump of a doll which they have found in some gutter of Paris. The whole thing is irresistibly comical, but so utterly unlike the Passage des Fleurs or the Avenue des Champs Elysées, that our tourist begins to doubt if he is really in Paris.

Suddenly the figure of a little hump-backed girl catches his eye, as those poor little creatures always do catch our eyes, and he watches her as she moves somewhat painfully along, talking eagerly to a boy at her side. Though not dressed in rags, they are evidently poor children, for the deformed girl's black dress is worn, and even the dainty ribbon round her neck shows signs of having been washed, and the boy's curly locks are protected by no hat. Evidently they are bound for some place, and the hawkers are to them so common a sight that they do not even notice them. But, wonder of wonders ! what is the child carrying? Surely it cannot be a Bible, in the midst of a Parisian rag-fair ! But a Bible it evidently is, for the sun falls at that moment on the gilt title; and no less plainly is it a Testament which half protrudes from the pocket of the boy's jacket. Our tourist, who is not a bad fellow at bottom, rubs his eyes, and asks himself if it is possible that in Paris too children go to Sunday-school at half-past nine in the morning; and finally, like a wise man, resolves to follow up the scent. The tram-line seems to lead on interminably up a badly-paved road, bordered with ill-conditioned-looking houses; but the children march steadily on, one or two others, somewhat less civilised-looking than they, joining them, and our friend follows. At the corner of a lane, strewn with refuse of all kinds, his eye falls on a young man in a battered straw hat, just setting down a little girl he had been carrying, who now proceeds to walk up the street with him, but with difficulty, for she too is a cripple. A little farther on, he finds himself in the middle of quite a large group of children, mostly neatly dressed, and all holding little books in their hands, who are dancing about irrepressibly in front of a building with the shutters up, whose sign bears in gigantic letters, "Réunions Populaires." A tall thin youth is exchanging badinage with the boys, and a somewhat older man, very poorly clad, is talking to a bright-eyed little woman, round whose skirts various little ones are clinging. Just as our friend reaches them, a shout is raised of some name which he does not catch, and the whole mass of children dart down the street, and precipitate themselves upon him of the straw hat, catching him by the arm, the leg, the coat-tail, anywhere in fact, some even covering his hand with kisses, or laying their heads caressingly against it, and so they escort him back in triumph. The thin youth at the door goes off into fits, being restrained by nothing but a sense of his own dignity from turning a somersault; but the bright-eyed woman darts a keen glance at the stranger, and seems to say something to the cripple's companion.

Feeling himself observed, our friend modestly makes a feint of walking on, and when he next turns round he sees, to his surprise, that all things are *in statu quo :* the children are still at the door, and all the others have disappeared. Suddenly a little boy flings himself down flat at the door, and peeping in underneath (for the clay floor is much worn), keeps his companions *au courant* with what is passing within. "They're bringing out the blackboard!" he shouts. "They're cleaning it!" "They're talking!" This in a tone of just indignation, private conversation being a clear waste of time. "Oh, they've got pictures!" "There's the door-key! they're praying! whisht!" and a slight hush falls on the motley crew. "He's coming!" and up gets the spy in a twinkling, and finds time to execute an impromptu dance before the door is flung open and the pavement cleared. A turn along the street promising nothing of interest to our tourist, he again finds himself below the gigantic "Réunions Populaires," and this time is fairly hooked by the bright-eyed woman, who seems told by instinct when to look out at the door. Responding courteously to her invitation, he enters and sits down. Before him are a clean, bright, well-proportioned hall, capable of seating some hundred and fifty people, the walls hung with large texts in silver and red, and the side opposite the door partially occupied with a platform of rough deal, on which are placed an organ, a slight desk also of rough wood, and a blackboard. About half the seats are occupied by children, who are at the moment repeating in concert several verses of Scripture, with that peculiar precision so noticeable among the little Parisians. A hymn follows, and then a Bible-lesson, both directed by the possessor of the straw hat, who indeed, so far as this Sunday-school is concerned, seems a pluralist of the most pronounced type. But the children absorb all the visitor's attention, they are so excessively eager. No need to tell them to watch the teacher while they are singing; they know the words already by heart, and snatch up the smallest gesture at once. And then the Bible-lesson! It is true the mere reading of the words, coveted honour though it is, does not seem to convey much idea to their minds, but when it is recapitulated with comments, and especially when a few leading points are put down on the board, the black eyes are all intelligence, and answers, or even volunteer observations, come so fast, that one would say the teacher had no need of preparation, the children expound the passage for themselves. Nobody even thinks of going to sleep, and the inevitable baby in night-cap and dirty frock is so carried away by the general enthusiasm, that he sucks his thumb complacently and forgets to howl. Everybody is sorry when the hour comes to an end, and the closing prayer is listened to with attention and reverence. Then begins the going out, but only begins, for though the large majority depart, some obscure but well-understood principle seems to detain others in twos and threes, who chat together quietly till their turn comes to be spoken to by the teacher or his lady assistant. One proceeds to gather up the hymn leaflets, another sorts out a miscellaneous collection of little stamped cards, another washes the blackboard, and all is done as quietly and orderly as though the school had existed for generations, though in reality it is barely six weeks old.

"At last!" I hear some reader exclaim. "Now, perhaps, we are going to hear how the children founded a meeting." Precisely so, my dear friend, but apocryphal though the foregoing pages look, they are none the less useful for showing how and why the children set to work. Topographically, Montreuil is connected with Père La Chaise; in actual fact, it is far more intimately united with the Bastille and the Faubourg St. Antoine. In Paris, as in all great cities, civilisation is gradually pushing the workman out from the centre, and so the cabinet-makers of St. Antoine are retiring year by year up the Rue de Montreuil. Within the barrier the more successful of them stay, but the unfortunate and the dissipated cross it, and discouraged, like our friend, at the long road they have to traverse before reaching Montreuil proper, they stop half-way, and sink deeper and deeper in misery and shame in some of the wretched hovels of Petit Montreuil, and become *gens de Cayenne*, inhabitants of Botany Bay. Such has for the last twenty years been the course of events ; there are, of course, many respectable people in Little Montreuil, many who have been born and bred in the township, but the majority are the offscourings of the Faubourg St. Antoine and the Rue de Charonne. Within the last few years, however, a new element has been at work in this faubourg, and something more than rascality and revolutionism has been carried out to Montreuil. An old *café*, ill-smelling and dirty, in the very centre of this ill-smelling and dirty *quartier*, has to many been the birthplace of a new life, pure and fragrant as God's own heaven. " La Conférence " has proclaimed the Gospel to hundreds of stalwart workmen and hunger-pinched children, and in not a few families "the meeting " is as essential a part of the household life, as " the kirk " is to your pious Scotch farmer.

And so it came to pass that when the superintendent of the St. Antoine Sunday-school was tearing down the Rue d'Avron (as the upper part of the long coach route is called) one afternoon in late spring, he heard his name shouted behind him, and looking round, beheld a lost pupil of the aforesaid school capering with joy at the rediscovery of his teacher. " But I haven't my meeting," was almost his first remark ; "where is *la conférence ?* " and his bright countenance fell sadly when he was told there was none in that region. " But you'll come, won't you? " he added eagerly, clinging to his friend's hand ; " you know it's too far to go back to St. Antoine, and you mustn't leave us without a meeting," and only a promise to do what could be done gave release from the loving though dirty little paw. Such a request could not but linger in the superintendent's mind, the more as his attention had long been directed to this *quartier* by the frequent disappearance in its direction of his friends in other parts of Paris. But only two months before, a fruitless search for an empty shop in this very street had induced the mission authorities to abandon formally all attempt to open a *salle* in the Rue de Montreuil. Nevertheless, not many days passed before the missionary was there again, this time closeted with a well-tried friend, the bright-eyed woman of the earlier pages. A few weeks before, she had, for the same reasons as the others, removed to Montreuil with her husband, and from her sympathy and sound advice were certain. She was not surprised to hear of the request of little Henri, for other children of the place to whom she talked had often said the same to her. When she spoke to them of Jesus, and told them stories she had heard in the meetings, they would ask, " But why don't you bring a meeting here, then? We'd like to hear that too." Could nothing be done? Perhaps something might, but there was no use going to the authorities with an indefinite proposal. Were there any empty shops to let in the neighbourhood? Yes, there were two, one on each side of the fortifications. So, after a little prayer, off went the two friends, *salle*-hunting. Disappointment! The one was much too small, the other outrageously dear. " Are there no others? " asked the missionary. " None that I know of," replied his friend, discouragedly. " Then there's nothing more to do." " Unless you would look in on Eugénie ; she'd be so glad to see you." " Ah yes, let us go ! " And down a bye-street they plunged, and into a court, and at last got inside a very small room, where a woman was serving a man, seated at a small table, with potatoes and gravy, and a very small child was standing solemnly surveying a chair which it had just knocked down. The hungry man was requested to continue his dinner, the child was beguiled from further attacks on the furniture by the offer of a piece of sugar, and conversation was begun with the mother. In a few minutes a step was heard in the court, and a little girl entered, all

crooked and bent, for she had fallen when an infant, and
hopelessly injured her back. She recognised quite well
both visitors, though she had left the St. Antoine meeting
very soon after its present director had come to it; and
every one felt at ease at once. " You're going to open a
meeting here, then?" she said confidently. " What makes
you think so, Eugénie?" asked her friend. " We have just
been trying to find a hall, but have had to give up in
despair." " Oh no," said she, confidently; "don't give up;
you're sure to get a hall, for I've asked God to give us one,
and He *always* hears our prayers."

" You are right, Eugénie," said the missionary. " I was
wrong to give up hope. Let us kneel down again and ask
God to find us a hall." And so the scheme was set on its
feet again, so to speak, and another prayer went up from
the miserable hovel that the children's wish might be
granted.

Soon after, the matter was mentioned to the central
mission authorities, but received with as much disfavour as
any proposal for the extension of the Gospel could be
received by such men. The mission staff was reduced, the
time of year unfavourable, the distance from the central
offices enormous; the thing should wait for a while at least.
But within a week the bright-eyed woman brought a new
piece of news. A wine-merchant, wholesale and retail,
established in the very centre of Petit Montreuil, was giving
up the retail part of his business, and with it his shop, or
saloon, and was of course perfectly ready to treat with anybody for the use of the premises. Here was a possible
salle, and out goes our missionary again. The place is
found to be exceedingly suitable, and the rent not
excessive; but before mentioning the matter to the authorities, he bethinks himself of another friend, living not far
off, and zealous exceedingly for the extension of Christ's
name. If he could be got to promise his help, might not

the difficulty of workers be overcome? and that same eager little woman is commissioned to approach him on the subject. Meanwhile, on leaving the dignified wine-merchant's, a very small child presents herself to the two friends, and asks calmly, " *Quand est-ce?* " It is one of the already partially instructed little ones, but the omen is good.

And now formal overtures can be made to the heads of the Mission. A convenient *salle*, not too dear, but of which the entry must be immediate, three workers already pledged to conduct the meetings, and, lastly, offers from these workers themselves to see to the fitting up of the building with their own hands, barring painter and plumber work, which men on the spot could do. And so at last Eugénie and her friends could be told that the meeting was coming. Nor did they lay any restraint on their tongues, and soon *la conférence* became the talk of the whole township, and even tramway conductors might be heard explaining to inquisitive travellers what the huge *enseigne* " Réunions Populaires " meant, explaining doubtless with more fluency than exactness, but still repeating more or less correctly what their children had told them. And so at last, on the 28th July, the *salle* was opened, and the children's wish was granted.

And it is curious the sort of propriety they seem to feel in it. In many of our adult meetings a large part of the audience consists of children, who come in more or less at haphazard, and listen or sleep as the notion takes them. But at Montreuil noticeably few come to the adult meeting, and these have all the air (unconsciously, of course) of delegates. They come in firmly and deliberately, in good time, and seat themselves well forward, where they listen with an eager, almost critical, air, turning round occasionally to judge by the countenances of the rest of the audience how they appreciate the good things that have

9

been provided for them with such difficulty. They never dream of leaving before the close ; on the contrary, they occasionally reserve a seat for some acquaintance whose work or other duties oblige him to come in late, and give their hand to their friend the missionary at the door with a very cordial grasp. " Courage, comrade !" they seem to say ; "our work is taking good hold." To their own meeting their attachment is passionate. One little boy whose father was proposing to take him to the hippodrome bargained that in any case he should be back in time for his " little meeting," and when, in spite of all his efforts, he arrived late, he refused to eat his dinner, in order that he might at least not miss " the big one."

The Thursday staff here has never numbered more than three, even when the audience is a hundred and fifty or a hundred and sixty, but our friend of the straw hat has had helpers sent him for Sunday morning, as efficient as any of his colleagues in England or Scotland could desire. Unfortunately ten o'clock is rather too early an hour for many of these poor children, who have to take the mother's place in preparing dinner or looking after the little ones, and the attendance, though steady, might be larger. An advanced class, however, of some twenty members held on Sunday evening, just before the ordinary meeting, makes up so far for what is lacking in the morning, and gives its teacher much pleasure.

Perhaps, before leaving Montreuil, a little glimpse might be given of the very real dangers from which God delivers us often in these lawless districts. Most frequently we know nothing either of the danger or of the deliverance ; in this case both were plain, and though the story has often been told in public both in

England and in America, it is striking enough to bear retelling.

The " Botany birds " of Montreuil of course looked at this Gospel work begun among them with no kindly eye, and threatened openly to put an end to it. Some two months after the opening of the hall, the three workers, on reaching the *salle*, were informed with much alarm by the concierge that she had overheard certain well-known lawless characters agree to come in that night by twos and threes, and at a given signal rise and destroy everything. It was too late to appeal for help from the police, even had we cared to do so, and help was asked only from Heaven. Then the doors were opened as usual, and shortly after the address began, ill-conditioned-looking fellows began to drop in by twos and threes, and seat themselves together in a far-away corner. The speaker was beginning to wonder when the signal would be given, when suddenly the door opened again, and a very different visitor came within the curtain. A gendarme, in his conspicuous white-braided uniform and jingling spurs and sabre, had left home, as he thought, at the usual hour, to report himself at the police-station, when it occurred to him on passing our lantern, almost the only good light at that time in the street, to look at his watch, and he found he was a quarter of an hour too soon. He made no difficulty, therefore, in accepting the invitation of our man, and walked into the *salle*. The Bible-woman motioned him to a seat, but he declined, saying he might have to leave suddenly, and standing back against the wall, involuntarily clinked his sword and spurs together. Round turned the *voyons* instantly, and recognising the officer of law, they sank back

resignedly in their seats with folded arms, and moved
only to leave when the meeting had terminated. " Nice
set of fellows these !" was all the gendarme said as
they passed out at the door; but even he was struck
when he was told from what in all probability we had
been saved through his timely appearance.

Let these two schools then serve as a sample of the
work we are doing. From the very beginning Mr. and
Mrs. McAll strove to teach the young as well as the
old, and if the work has now largely fallen into other
hands, it is because the development of so great a
work required that the different departments should
become more and more specialised. Our opportunity
is this : on the one side, God's name must not be
pronounced in the public schools, nor His Bible read
as a basis for moral teaching ; on the other, the
children, as yet largely uncontaminated, feel the need
of a God, and love to study His Word. We meet
therefore a felt want, and we have but to show that
the knowledge and love of God produce a change of
heart and life to have the parents, even the pro-
fessedly infidel among them, on our side. And though,
alas ! many of even our best pupils slip away gradually
from our grasp, largely owing, I am convinced, to
defective organisation, even these have got correct *head*-
knowledge, if nothing more, and cannot go about pro-
pagating or even pretending to believe the hideous
nonsense that their fathers accept as truth. Much yet
remains to be done, through Young Men's Christian
Association and Young Women's Christian Association
agencies, through Bible Unions, and especially through
a more living, hearty Church relationship, to carry
on and complete what is done in our schools and

Bible-classes; but a solid foundation is being laid, and in due time a stately edifice will be reared thereupon. If throughout the Mission twice every week 7,000 children are being gently urged to come to Christ, and at least half that number getting besides systematic and continuous instruction in Bible history and doctrine, we may, I think, say that our work, though small in comparison with what should be done, is large enough to make its importance felt, and hopeful enough to command the sympathy of all God's people. And though we may seem to some to move slowly, we remember that that has been the motto of the Mission from the first; every new procedure must be well tested before it is adopted, and our agents should be well trained before they are set to work. If the ideal agency of a well-appointed Sunday and week-day school, with infant, middle, and advanced departments, flanked by Young Men's and Young Women's Christian Associations, Tract Distributers' Union, Musical Society, and Library, be scarcely attained, yet in any even of our Paris *salles* are we to regard the conscientious teaching of the Gospel even to a sadly fluctuating audience of no importance? A thousand times no! Because we have a goal before us, do we neglect the road thither? Till we can have the complete article, shall we cast aside the first made shapings? The *faithful* servant was the one to receive commendation, not he who worked according to the newest methods or with the completest set of tools, intellectual or material; and faithful to the Master is what even the humblest children's worker of the McAll Mission struggles to be.

CHARLES E. GREIG.

"TELL ME THE OLD, OLD STORY."

IMITATED BY R. SAILLENS.

Redites-moi l'histoire
De l'amour de Jésus ;
Parlez-moi de la gloire
Qu'il promet aux élus.
J'ai besoin qu'on m'instruise,
Car je suis ignorant ;
Qu'à Christ on me conduise
Comme un petit enfant.

CHŒUR.   Redites-moi l'histoire,
Redites-moi l'histoire,
Redites-moi l'histoire,
De l'amour de Jésus !

Redites-moi l'histoire
De la crèche à la croix ;
Eveillez ma mémoire,
Oublieuse parfois.
Cette histoire si belle,
Dites-la simplement ;
Elle est toujours nouvelle,
Répétez-la souvent.
Redites-moi, etc.

Redites-moi l'histoire
De mon divin Sauveur ;
C'est lui dont la victoire
Affranchit le pécheur.
Ce glorieux message,
Oh ! redites-le moi,
Lorsque je perds courage,
Lorsque faiblit ma foi.
Redites-moi, etc.

Redites-moi l'histoire,
Quand le monde trompeur
Me vend sa vaine gloire
Au prix de mon bonheur.
Et quand, loin de la terre,
Je prendrai mon essor,
En fermant la paupière,
Que je l'entende encor !
Redites-moi, etc.

VI.

FRENCH WORK FOR CHRISTIAN LADIES.

BY MRS. GEORGE THEOPHILUS DODDS.

IS there much work for ladies to do in the Mission ?
And if there is, what is it ?

These questions are not surprising, for it is not so
long ago that they were asked, rather doubtfully, within
the Mission itself. It is quite true that woman's influence was interwoven with the work from its very
foundation. We need not discuss the question whether
Mr. McAll *could* have confronted these cynical Parisians,
could have melted and won them, had he been alone.
He was not called to attempt so hard a task. There
was a gentle, hopeful, helpful spirit ever at his side.
To her the musical part of the programme, which has
so greatly contributed to the success of the whole, owes
in great part its execution. Busied not only in teaching to unaccustomed voices the holy songs, but in
giving shape musically to the very songs themselves,
the hymn-book grew under her hand from half a dozen
leaves to the large collection of nearly three hundred
hymns now so familiar to most of us.

In the first days of the Mission, Mrs. McAll had
usually a young friend and amanuensis to help her.
They, with a few friends who gathered round, formed

GEORGE THEOPHILUS DODDS.
PASTEUR ECOSSAIS
COLLÈGUE DU REV R.W. MACALL
DANS LA MISSION POPULAIRE
ÉVANGELIQUE DE FRANCE

TOMB OF THE LATE REV. G. T. DODDS, IN PASSY CEMETERY, PARIS.

the choir in every meeting, knew all the people by sight, kept in order all the books, besides doing a hundred nameless things to help.

As the meetings got more numerous, the lady helpers increased in number, but their occupations continued much the same. Nine years ago I remember the small room where two or three of them spent their mornings, armed with paste and brushes, preparing large-lettered texts, binding books, and repairing those that had been returned in bad condition from the growing libraries.

When a new hall was to be got ready all was bustle to adorn its walls suitably, to hasten lazy workmen and concierges, to do the sweeping in person if it could not be got done in any other way. All these things were most needful in those days of slender resources. The same things are done still to a certain extent, along with other work which then had scarcely been attempted.

For, when all this was done, it only furnished work for a few. Woman's work seemed more like the drop of oil to keep the machine going smoothly than like part of the vast machine itself. To many, indeed, Mr. McAll's very calling seemed to a certain extent to preclude woman's work. Pressed in the spirit to bring the Gospel to bear *at once* on the multitudes of France, it was strong men's voices that he needed. The sowing was too broadcast, on too vast a scale, to be attempted by a woman's hand. So many argued.

And yet by the year 1877 (at which point my personal knowledge begins) higher work was opening up for women. They began to rally round the Mission of their own accord, drawn as if by an irresistible attraction. They sought out the poor in their homes, and found a welcome beyond all anticipation. Among them were Misses Matheson and Coldstream, whose disinterested devotion to the work has formed ever since a most valuable element in its spiritual development.

But it was not easy for such friends as these to find a suitable residence. And their numbers were all too few. My thoughts used to turn wistfully to Scotland, with its well-ordered ranks of teachers and visitors of all sorts. Visions of mothers' meetings, schools, and classes flitted across my brain. Would they ever be realised? It was a case where only the supply could prove whether the demand existed or not.

Now these visions have been more than realised, and still the demand is unappeased.

The " Maison Bonar" (Home for Lady-workers).

Among others, the motherly heart of one friend* took in the needs of the case. Visiting Paris in the year of the Exposition (1878), she yearned over the multitudes who had no one to say a friendly word in sickness or sorrow. Besides this, she was touched by the privations of one or two ladies who had left bright English homes to live at the top of five dark, well-worn stairs in a Belleville house, each *alone*, with one room and a kitchen in which she could just turn round to cook her own frugal meal. How dreary, she thought, to creep up those stairs on a frosty night, weary with a day's work, to find no light, no fire, except what her numbed fingers could kindle, no one to speak to,

---

* Mrs. Horatius Bonar, called up higher in December, 1884.

nothing to be done but to heat some comforting drink
by the lamp and go to rest. These pioneer workers
were happy, no doubt. I have hardly ever seen any one
engaged in the work who did not enjoy it thoroughly.
They had found their way to the hearts of the people,
and had many friends outside their narrow rooms.
But yet, from the outside, such a life looked hard and
dreary. It was not a life which one could ask any
young and inexperienced lady to undertake. And the
only alternative to this was an ordinary French
pension, whose cost would in many cases exceed the
means of the worker, and where she would find herself
far less free than in her solitary rooms.

Some got over these difficulties by the plan of living
two and two. But the thought occurred, "Why not
more than two ? Why not have a little house ? "

It was not at first easy to see the way to this.
Some asked, as I have told you, " Where is the work
for so many ladies ? " others, " Where are the ladies
to come from ? " others, " Where is the money ? "
" And then the house ? " " And the furniture ? "
" And the management ? "—since Mr. and Mrs. McAll
could not themselves be at the head—and " Could so
many ladies live together without quarrelling ? "

By the good hand of our God upon us, all these difficulties were smoothed away. Our dear one went back
to Scotland full of the project. In several well-tried
friends, mostly English, she thought she had found
ladies who might live and work in Paris. And she was
right. And she found courage to write to a few liberal
givers, asking them to entrust her with a round sum,
guaranteed for three years. Her appeal was at once
responded to. The hunt on our part for a suitable

house followed, and the first Home was found in Rue Ampère, close to Courcelles Station.

All this happened just seven years ago this month—in October of 1879. In these seven years the Home has been changed several times, and so have many of its occupants. Some have remained steadfast; some have hived off to other parts of Paris; few have left the work altogether, for even those whose duties lie in England return now and again, whenever they have opportunity.* The loving house-mother was the first to leave, to our great regret, on account of health, but a successor has always been found; the continuity of the Home has never been broken; none of the shocks or difficulties which were predicted have occurred; and thanks, under God, to a few faithful friends, who shall be nameless here, though never forgotten, we have never wanted for money.

The Home only furnishes a *pied-à-terre*, as the French call it, for workers who have a difficulty in living elsewhere. The more each "lady" can live among her people in this district or in that, and so diffuse the good influence, the more efficient she will be likely to be. Ten years ago the lady-workers numbered some half-dozen; now they are counted by the score. And again, the question arises, "What do all these ladies do?"

---

* Mrs. Ponsonby-Moore was the first to fill this post. The names of Misses Matheson, Coldstream, Grimstone, Moggridge, Wilkinson, Johnstone, are all well-known. They were among the earliest inmates.

The Home is now situated at No. 21, Rue de l'Arc de Triomphe, and the fund is in the hands of the Rev. Dr. Bonar and the present writer.

Their work has so many sides that I am at a loss how to begin to tell it.

I will begin with that easiest, simplest, most powerful of agencies, *a kind word spoken.*

A woman looked into one of the halls one evening. She was still young, but crushed and miserable-looking. Her soul was bitter against all the world and against God, most of all against her own husband. He had disappointed her, and even in their far-off country home they had been alienated. Out of work and wretched, their life had been one of mutual recrimination. But the last drop of bitterness was when he proposed going to seek work in Paris. "I will never go," she said. "You *shall* go," said her own mother; "he is your husband, and you must stick to him." They went, but found no work, no bread, worst of all no love or peace. Alone in the wide strange city, without a crumb of comfort in all her life, the poor creature drooped. As she stopped a moment to listen and pass on, a lady spoke to her. It was not much, but "it was the first kind word anybody had spoken to me since I came to Paris three months ago. It broke me down altogether." So she came back, and back again, drawn by an irresistible power to the place. One day she told her husband, "I have found a religion that has done me good; I am sure it would do you good too. Come with me, and I will show you." He came, and now all is changed. There is work, and bread, and love in their home; they are helpers of one another's joy in Christ. She says, "I thought my being forced to come to Paris was the worst thing that had ever happened to me, and God made it the very best." Truly, "a word spoken in season, how good it is."

The Doorkeeper.

But the ·doorkeeper has many duties. Let Miss Moggridge describe them :—

" I explain, for the benefit of strangers, that a door-keeper, *portière*, or *dame de la porte*, is a lady charged, in one or more of Mr. McAll's halls, with the multifarious offices of *inner* gatekeeper, deputy hostess, hall policeman and superior, tract and Testament-distributer, general informant, and, later on, friend and visitor to those who accept the invitation handed them at the door, and enter. As a rule, the authority of the lady is recognised politely, and often amusingly appealed to. 'I do wish you would speak to this gentleman, madam,' says a Shakespearian-looking individual. ' He is muttering so loud, I cannot hear the preacher. It is too bad ! Could you not put him out ?' In the speaker the lady recognises one who had himself ' been spoken to ' and threatened a few nights ago with ' putting out,' but now his·soul is thirsty, and his thirst must be quenched. ' Putting out ' is much dreaded as disgrace. Generally a little persuasion or a few marked words suffice. ' Your young friend is fresh from the country, I observe ; you should teach him to sing better,' is said to the neighbour of a giddy, well-attired young gentleman, who is doing his best to perplex the singers and amuse his comrades. 'Oh no, not so, I assure you, madam,' is the reply. ' Pardon me, sir ; no *Parisian* could sing or behave so badly.' The young man is quenched, for every Parisian piques himself on being an accomplished man

of the world. . . . A young workman whispers softly,
'What was the number of the *cantique* just sung,
madam ? ' 'It was No. 14—" Sinner, return."'
'That's it! I want to buy a book with that *cantique*
in it.' He gets one for twopence. . . . In the smaller
halls the people get personally attached to their lady.
'If you abandon us, *we* shall abandon you,' they say.
'Her sympathetic face attracts us,' is the reason
given for fuller attendances when 'the lady' is among
them. . . . And as she hands Gospel after Gospel
to the eager claimants passing out, answering questions
and exchanging friendly greetings, which lead to visits,
Bible-readings, prayer, and conversions, she feels that
though neither an 'orator,' a president, nor a chief
musician, she is still, by the favour of God, a '*helper*
in the war' carried on in the McAll halls against sin,
and ignorance, and unbelief, a 'helper' on the way
to those who, perhaps, slowly and with difficulty, are
drawing nigh to the feet of that Saviour, Jesus, so
long hidden, and now so freely lifted up before their
eyes." *

The Organist.

Next in order comes the leading of the song. Each
of the hundred and forty meetings held weekly in and
round Paris requires an organist, and depends largely

---

* Instances often come to our knowledge in which the kind
manner of a lady in offering a hymn-book to a stranger entering
the mission-hall, or a Scripture portion or tract on leaving it,
has formed a first link in awakening interest and the desire to
return. In a very remarkable letter containing the personal
testimony of a workman at the Rue de Rivoli, dated November,
1885, he uses these expressions : " A lady who stood at the door
(*I would rather say, an angel*) put into my hand a little **tract**

upon her for its success. The work is delightful in itself, a delight to the skilful musician as her fingers wander over the keys of the charming instrument which Mrs. McAll has chosen for some large hall, and as the swell of sweet enthusiastic voices rises around her ; it is no less a joy to the timid player, who can but just play the tune upon some very indifferent harmonium in a poor quarter, to teach the lovely hymns to a group of children, or to lead a band of poor men and women.

Passing through a low quarter of Paris—I think it was that named after Voltaire—a gentleman saw a group of a dozen or more children, sitting on a squalid stair, while their voices rang clear and sweet—

> Avançons-nous joyeux, toujours joyeux,
> Vers le pays des esprits bienheureux.

That hymn finished, another and another followed from the cheerful little chorus. It was as if they could never be tired of singing. As words and melody rang through the gloomy tenement one might hope that, as to Paul and Silas, "the prisoners were listening to them."

Had there been no mission-school, what would these children have been singing ? Perhaps a snatch of the latest opera, more likely some stupid and vulgar couplet reiterated *ad nauseam*, very likely nothing at all. France has few sweet, pure secular songs, like those of Scotland and Germany.

---

named 'The Prisoner.'" He goes on to say that he at first had despised the little book and determined not to read it, but, finding himself some days after without occupation, he read it, and found his own history there, and was led to ask himself, "What can I do to enter the kingdom of heaven, with such a burden of guilt and so many stains ?" He returned to our mission-room, and there he found Christ.—R. W. M.

And so Voltaire is outwitted for once in his own quarter. He only made books for the people; he left to Mr. and Mrs. McAll to make their songs!

The Bureau.

I simply mention the work of the bureau, or business-office of the Mission, because some one must attend to it. It is in good hands just now, the hands of Madame Soltau, *née* Monod. With this I class the miscellaneous jobs which fall to the lot of all in turn, such as changing and keeping in order the books for lending in the different halls, procuring and distributing tracts, keeping accounts, tying up parcels, keeping the concierges and *employés* about the halls up to their work, etc. One lady also is charged to supply all the doors, another all the organs, and so on. That nothing may run into confusion, a committee of ladies meets to arrange all these matters.

Some of this sounds, and *is*, very "secular," and it repels some. I do not know, I hardly think, that it would have repelled the great Apostle who made tents with his own hands that he might not be chargeable to the Churches. One may generally test the value of a worker by her willingness to do *anything* that offers.

And we, at a distance, can hardly imagine the influence that is gained by the fact that *ladies* should do all these things. To come, wet or dry, hot or cold, to the appointed place, organ, or door, or library; to hand a book; to guide a tottering creature to a comfortable seat; to find the place in a hymn-book; to answer a bewildered question,—these things are little in themselves, but they prove to these poor people that we are *willing* to serve them. " Nothing for nothing " has been the rule of the only Church they know, the Church that in France, whatever may be the case elsewhere, has driven the poor from its very confessionals to feed upon the rich.   And so the contrast strikes them at once, and the amazement never ends that a lady should take all this trouble, and for nothing !

"Why do these people do it ?"   "Who pays all this ?"   And various the conjectures in return. "Rothschild pays for it," says one (again we quote Miss Moggridge).   "No; it is the Gallican Church," says another.   "I tell you they are Protestants," says a woman.   "No, they are Jews," says her husband. "Anyhow it is true, and does one good," says a third. I have even heard Mr. McAll credited with a large *fortune*, which he spends upon the *réunions*.   But then the puzzle remains, "Why does he do it ?"   "How much to pay ? " says a countryman before resting his limbs on the proffered chair.   "Nothing."   "How much to pay ? " as, anxious to join in the sweet strain, he yet hesitates to take the proffered hymn-book.   "Nothing." "How much to pay ? " he asks again on being handed a little Gospel and tract at the end of the meeting. "Nothing."   Gaping, he goes out, and unburdens himself to the man at the door.   "Well, see that ! and that ! and that ! and the chair, and the *cantique*, and the discourse, and the lady,—all for *nothing !   C'est moi qui suis content !* "

"I believe nothing," said a young mother of some education to me as she bent over her baby.   Yet she sang the child to sleep with *cantiques* and found a strange fascination in the meetings.   "I was brought up in a convent," she continued, "and before I was twelve years old, I found out that the religion of the

Sœurs was a 'comedy.' Now I wish I could believe, but it all sounds to me like nonsense. But "—and here her tone changed to deep seriousness—" I at least see that you people of the Mission believe what you say " (" Vous êtes des gens convaincus "). It was little, and yet it was a seed which perhaps might spring up in God's own time.

I may seem to have told this story out of place ; but the train of thought which led me to it is this : who knows what had led that woman to conclude that with us faith was a reality ? Not the words and tone of the speaker alone, however earnest ; the conduct, the sympathy, the loving self-denial of the feeblest and youngest helper there, I am sure, had something to do with it. Religion in France has been too often *disproved* by the conduct of its teachers. It must be proved now in the same way. Mere talk is nothing to these people ; they know how easy it is. But the simplest word or action becomes significant to them if it means the patient and loving giving of one's life-service to people who have no claim upon one. *That*, they feel, is something they cannot understand. There must be something in it when things go as far as that !

Sunday-schools.

The modes of work I have been describing require neither a very full French vocabulary, nor much of what people call a " gift." Therefore they are the most suitable for beginners. But some, consciously or unconsciously, have the talent for imparting what they know. To such a limitless field is open. And to begin again with the simplest, there is the Sunday-school, or the Thursday-school, which is the same thing.

I am not going to describe these,—first, because Mr. Greig is well able to plead his own cause; and, secondly, because you all know what Sunday-schools are at home. Emerging from an irregular and difficult infancy, the schools of Paris are fast attaining the normal standard of organisation and efficiency. *Some* of them, indeed, are *more* efficient than any school I ever saw in this country. Some are not, and this for the reason that *teachers cannot be had.* The difficulty of keeping up the supply is something which cannot be imagined in England. Think of it, and then remember that the mission-school may be the child's *only chance* of ever hearing the name of God seriously spoken, of ever knowing what Christ did for him. Such knowledge is forbidden in the public schools.

Mothers' Meetings.

Next I name the mothers' meetings, or *ouvroirs*, as they are often called. These are very successful in the poorer districts, and gather together, not so much the younger mothers, who are generally out at work, but the old and infirm, the out-of-work, often the respectable but slowly starving poor; their bodies are provided for as well as their souls. Madame Dalencourt's excellent plan is followed of doling out vegetables and groceries at a little under cost price. Materials for clothing are sold in the same way, wool is *given* for knitting, and they knit or sew while an interesting book is being read. Then the work is laid on the lap while a chapter of the Bible is explained, and prayer is offered. Singing enlivens the whole. Often a cup of tea or coffee is added; and three hours of an afternoon are spent happily as by a little family gathered together.

Of course, this programme varies very much according to the place. In well-to-do districts nothing is *given;* in some places the women simply come to listen, their own sewing in hand. But in general these meetings give scope for very various gifts : from weighing, measuring, and cutting out, to clear and intelligent reading aloud, or prayer and explaining God's Word.

And now, although I could say much more, I must simply leave the rest of the details for the reader to fill up. The dispensary, with its mighty agency for good ; the classes for girls and young women, who often need to be caught with guile in the shape of a sewing class or a course of English, concluded with reading and prayer ; the little inner circles formed in the different classes for those who have learned to love prayer and the study of God's Word ; the Christmas-trees ; the tea-meetings ; and much more, I leave out, not because it is unimportant, but because it may be imagined. And if there be any other form of work which you, my reader, have found useful in England, it is most likely that it too may have its place across the Channel. And, oh, how delightful must be the feelings of the lady who introduces any of these for *the first time* in a new quarter, for they were almost all unknown (even Christmas-trees) outside the narrow circle of Protestant members until a few years ago.*

The Visitor.

But I cannot thus pass over the visitor's work, for to it everything else leads. Doorkeeper, organist, teacher, the *dame de la réunion,* whoever she may be, is sure to

* Twelve mothers' meetings are held weekly in Paris (inclusive of those of Madame Dalencourt, for which we gladly lend

be asked, nay *entreated*, to visit. Her clients may be
miles away ; they may live up long flights of separate
stairs in streets far from one another ; that does not
matter ; the welcome she receives makes up for all. So
she may go on and on till time and strength fail, and
then sit down in a kind of despair to pray for some one
to help her. And there is no one. All are as much
overwhelmed as herself.

Will you bear with me if I say that it makes me
angry when, in this favoured Scotland, I hear a Sunday-
school teacher complain that her scholars wander to three
schools in one day that they may lay claim to three
treats, or a district visitor sighing because a city
missionary and two or three ladies have been in her
district before her, and the people are overvisited, over-
talked to, overcharitied ? They have got so used to
being talked to, that they think they are conferring
quite a favour in listening ; they have caught hold of the
proper phrase, and know what to say in the right place.
I may be putting an extreme case ; I am certainly not
putting an unreal one. I can speak from personal
experience of the pain of a young girl set to do good to
people who knew the *outside* of Christian doctrine, and
that only.

" Overwrought," " Gospel-hardened," " overlapping
Societies "—what do these phrases mean ? They mean
valuable energies running to waste ; they mean heart-
burnings, and jealousies, and bitterness. They mean,
I am afraid, at bottom, that many of God's people are
not where the Master would have them to be.

---

our halls), attended by an average of nearly four hundred. In
addition, there are four young women's meetings weekly, with
about eighty members.

Now in France all this is reversed. People are touched and astonished when you seek them out. No one ever did so before, they say. And then they are so delightfully *naïve* in their ignorance. They don't in the least know how you expect them to talk, and therefore you get their real thoughts. The oddest sayings come out without their knowing that they are saying anything strange.

Their ignorance is saddening, but it gives you this advantage : that you know how to reply.

" No, I have never sinned," said a woman, indignantly. " To be sure," she added, " I have sometimes said my fish was fresh when it wasn't, but then God knew that was for my interest, and He will not blame me." " I have never done anything to merit so much suffering," is one of the commonest sayings. " What can that poor boy have done, that God should hate him so ? " said another, speaking of a poor boy who had met with a frightful accident.

In answer to my question whether she thought she would go to heaven, a hard-working mother replied, " Certainly. I have brought up eight children, and done my best for them, and they told me in the convent that a woman who did so had as much merit as a *religieuse.*" " I try to do all the good I can. I hope in that way to atone for some faults I have committed." " Don't tell me that my sufferings are not meritorious," cried a much-tried woman. " You take away the only consolation I have under them." Being told of the merits of the Saviour, she replied thoughtfully, " Yes, but it is possible to count too much on the merits of Jesus Christ."

Such are these people's real unvarnished thoughts about sin and salvation.

But oh, if in visiting one meets with things to sadden, there are discoveries which gladden the very heart. " I was brought up under the purest teaching," said a woman. " I was a Vaudoise, and I thought I knew Christ. But one evening, while Mr. Sautter was speaking, my eyes seemed suddenly opened. In a moment I saw the great, wonderful love of God in sending His Son to die for me, and I—oh, what a wretch I had been that I had never loved Him for it! I saw myself black, black, black. I could do nothing but weep. I went upstairs, threw myself on my bed, and cried to God nearly all night. In the morning God answered me, and I was calmed."

I should have liked to say a few words about *the unvisited*, those quite outside, the unchurched, the non-attendants at the meetings, the multitudes for whose soul no man cares. The visitor's heart aches for them, but she can do nothing for them, for she cannot over-take her own work. The pastor can do nothing for them, for he cannot overtake his work. The sister of charity has deserted them, because they will not come to Confession. The priest will never go near them till the time comes to bury them. No man cares for their souls. But upon this vast and terrible subject I dare not enter.

And now let my readers remember that while, for shortness' sake, I have spoken only of Paris, these forms of work are called for *all over France*. The great towns —Lyons, Marseilles, Bordeaux, etc.—have followed the example of Paris in every particular, while the smaller places imitate as best they may. Had I space to de-scribe the provincial work, it would prove deeply in-teresting. It affords also variety in the work, for many a lady whose health and circumstances do not suffer her to cast her lot in a large city finds her sphere in the smaller towns.

The Need.

A worker, writing to me, thus expresses himself: " I would say to the Christian public, Here are those years past of patient, careful, and often tearful preparation. Here are the results so far: an established mission, thousands of hearers, with unlimited openings for developing the work in all its branches, and the need, the urgent need,—always supposing the presence and blessing of God the Holy Ghost,—to go forward with a strong hand, and increase the existing modes of work, and develop many more. I cannot see any stronger claim. For real *deep need*, and for the truly open door, can we turn anywhere to find these rather than to France ? "

Here, then, is a nation that craves the Gospel faster than we can give it. And yet, while I write, tidings have reached me, that for want of funds Mr. McAll is likely to be forced to cut off stations and dismiss agents. It is like putting an already famished crew upon short allowance. I was asked the other day, " What *do* they want ? " I could not help replying, " They want *everything*, except *opportunities*." Only those who have experienced it can know the pain and trial of doing such a work as this *short-handed*.

There is something, after all, in the ambition to preach Christ where He has not been preached, so as not to build on another's foundation ! Some of us may have longed to do so, and yet have been restrained from crossing the ocean. It might, however, be in our power to cross the Channel. And if we cannot, perhaps we might be able to send a substitute. How pleasant to send out some Christian girl you know, following her steps with prayerful sympathy! What a link this would be to the sister country! Or to provide an evangelist, how blessed! For if there is work for women, there is no less work for men, strong, wise, consecrated men. "And how shall they preach except they be sent?" *

To-day!

The help we purpose to give must be given *to-day*. We have no time to dream over these things, and to wait for a convenient season. Everywhere in this nineteenth century ten years seem to do the work of a hundred. And no part of the world is changing more rapidly than France. While we are dreaming, the solid earth is heaving under our feet; to-morrow we may awake to find the face of all things changed. And then will our help be in vain? Or will it not be needed? In either case, it will be too late.

For when I speak of change, I can never forget the upward and the downward sense of the word, that transition does not of itself mean regeneration, nor the casting off of superstition, peace and holiness.

France has gone out in quest of a religion! Even men who want none for themselves often admit that the nation, if she is to be saved, must have one. Shall her quest end in a fall back into superstition?

---

* The sum of £50, £40, or even much less, would set many a valuable worker who has a *little* means of her own free to go. For an evangelist, generally from £150 up to £250 or £300 is needed.

Not likely. In Rationalism,—a religion without the supernatural? Or shall she give it up, and say, " No God"? Or—shall the pure Gospel enlighten her from end to end?

These questions we cannot answer. Only, we know that the nation we have been accustomed to call "Catholic France" exists no longer as such. It is in a state of fusion, and in the chaos, new forces of crystallisation are drawing the atoms now to this side, now to that. A purer faith,—a darker Atheism :— a new impulse from heaven of hope and progress,—a blast from hell, killing all faith, not only in God, but in the very names of faith and purity and virtue :—such are the alternatives. Such are the chemical solvents at work. And shall we calmly look on and watch the process till the molten mass has cooled, and the stamp is irreversible?

There has gone out a rumour in many quarters among those who may call themselves unbelievers, or who may call themselves Catholics, that there is a religion which reasonable men believe, and whose adherents are consistent with themselves. They pause to see if it is true. It is their last hope, as they turn their back on the old creeds, and their face to the gulf of infidelity. "Will this new thing deceive us, as the old did?" they ask wistfully. "Is it but a new form of the old, or is it anything which we may really believe and hold by? Is it, in short, a *reality*, or a name?" Life and death hang on the answer, and that answer they will not take from the *lips* of the Christian alone, but from his *life*.

In this light, it seems to me a most solemn responsibility even to pass through the country at this moment.

I confess I tremble when I think of the thousands who leave our shores for France annually with no object but to see and to enjoy. Even earnest Christians are apt to be off duty and off guard at such a time. And the French know that we profess something higher than they do. They know we profess to keep the Sabbath, and they watch to see if we do so. They know that we profess an active religion, and they watch to see if we will live in selfish, unloving isolation. They watch our Protestantism to see if it is *alive* and *true*. They have been deceived before; they will not be deceived again. And if this new *évangile* do not prove itself a living thing sent down from heaven, if it be full of cant and sham, like the rest, then it too shall be shot down with the rest of the rubbish of the past.

All hangs in the balance. Christian zeal and love are ripening. Blasphemy and evil of all kinds are ripening too. The fruit and the tares are growing together apace. We cannot prophesy the end. Shall the nation as a whole accept or reject, love or hate the offered Gospel? Only one thing we are sure of: that this is the day of the nation's visitation, that to it, as to Judea of old, the words are spoken, " Notwithstanding, be ye sure of this: the kingdom of God is come nigh unto you."

VII.

SOME STORIES OF OUR CHILDREN'S WORK.

Happy Death of a Parisian Girl.

YOU have asked me for some details of the death of a girl to whom God sent me to deliver His message. I can say that I have once more experienced the truth of those words of Jesus, "If thou wouldst believe, thou shouldest see the glory of God " (John xi. 40).

She never came to our meetings, but her mother, who has attended them for several months, had spoken a little about them to her, which made it easier for me to begin a religious conversation. Her mother, who had heard the truth, but without understanding it, authorised me nevertheless to tell her what would be the probable issue of her illness. The poor child wept bitterly, saying that she did not want to die, that she did not want to leave her poor mother. I continued to visit her every day, at her own express desire, and took her books, which she read with pleasure. One day, after having read her "Jessica's First Prayer," she said to me, "I have said to God, 'O God, grant that I may come to believe like this girl;'" but she always asked me to pray for her recovery. She was trusting to the doctor, who deceived her, and one day, when I told her so, she said to me, "Well, ask the doctor about it yourself, and come and tell me what he says." I did so, and when I told her that the doctor had no hope of her recovery,

she was very downcast; but a minute after she called me
to her, kissed me, and said, " Thank you. Will you pray
with me ? " I did so, and from that day she was always
ready to talk to me about her approaching death, but she
kept saying to me that she was not sure that her sins were
pardoned. Ultimately she became deaf, so that I could no
longer talk to her, and as she was too feeble to read, I
brought her small cards containing suitable verses of the
Bible ; these she read, putting them into a little box, which
she kept on her bed, that she might re-read them, and
calling them her "treasures." When I told her that one
was a prayer, she learnt it by heart, and repeated it in the
midst of her sufferings. She was particularly fond of "God
so loved the world," etc.

A week before her death she said to me, " Oh, madam,
I don't understand very much, but I know I am going to
die, and yet I am content, quite content in my heart," and
she smiled. " And your sins ? " I asked. " Oh, I know
now that I am forgiven ; I am going away, and I am happy,
but don't say anything to my poor mother; she would be
too sad."

After that day she still suffered a great deal, but she was
very patient, and wished me to be often near her, that she
might hear about Jesus and heaven. She was always
begging me to pray for her, and one evening, before leaving
her, I urged her to pray herself, to tell God all her thoughts,
and to leave herself in His hands. She thanked me, and
the next day—it was the evening before her death—she said
to her mother, " I wish to be alone to-day." When I came
in the morning, she pointed to heaven, smiling, and passed
the rest of the day in prayer. She seemed to have no
more need of me, and when I left she did not ask me to
come back, as she used to do every time I quitted her.
The next day—the day of her death—when she saw me she
said with a great effort—for it was only with difficulty that

she could speak—"I am perfectly happy." Two hours before her death she signed to me to give her her passages of Scripture. I gave her three of them, she took them in her hand and tried to read them, but her sight was already dim and nearly gone; she smiled and raised them to her lips. It was the last sign of consciousness she gave. She died in peace. The mother said to me, "If I had not been at Mr. McAll's meetings, I should not know whether my daughter is in heaven; but I am quite sure that she is happy."

They are Catholic, but they wished for a Protestant pastor, and accordingly M. Fallot conducted the funeral service. I have since learned that the brother tried to console his mother by reminding her of the comforting words which the pastor had spoken. On returning from the cemetery the landlady, a pious woman and a thorough Catholic, asked me a number of questions about what she had heard, and invited me to come to see her, and tell her about these things. I trust to induce her to come to our meetings.

J. JOUY.

The Infidel's Little Daughter at Pantin.

A little girl has been brought to Christ. For some time I observed her near the platform at each service. She was lame, and her mother used to bring her in a perambulator. She was thirteen years old, but so thin and deformed that she did not appear to be more than seven or eight. I was told that her infidel father frequently struck her when intoxicated, and she would crouch in a corner and weep. She would no doubt have been ruined by the evil influences with which she was surrounded if an accident had not altered the course of her life. One afternoon, on returning from school, as she was playing with her young companions, she slipped and fell receiving serious injuries. Fearing that she would be punished, she said nothing to her parents about it, and the injuries became worse and worse. During the many long days that the poor child was on her bed of suffering, she did not hear a single kind word from her parents. She was then taken to the Lutheran Deaconesses' House. While there, she underwent several operations with extraordinary courage. After a twelvemonth she returned to her parents, but the spiritual impressions received in the Deaconesses' House could not be effaced. In summer her mother allowed her to be brought to our children's services, but there was nothing that led me to think that she was a Christian. Soon afterwards a complication of diseases necessitated her being removed to the Catholic Hospital of the Child Jesus, where she remained two years. We cannot describe the intense suffering she passed through ; sleep fled from her, and a burning fever wearied her, but she told us afterwards that what grieved her most was that there was no one to tell her of Jesus ; but she prayed, and was thus comforted. One day the doctors gathered around her bed and thought there was no possible hope of her recovery ; she then asked to be sent back to her parents. Having returned home, the New Testament which a lady had presented to her became her constant companion, and through it she was led into the light of the Gospel. "Thou hast hid these things from the wise and prudent, and hast revealed them unto babes." Suddenly I heard that she was freed from all her pains. Her last words were, "I believe in Jesus my Saviour. I am saved. Stay near me to the end." The unhappy parents, still in unbelief and rebellion, could only say, "If there was a God, He would not have taken away our child." Our hope is that the same light which shone upon this little angel shall triumph over the darkness which envelops their souls. We continue to see them occasionally.

G. Van der Beken.

I heard, one Sunday evening, just a fortnight ago, that a child who attended the meeting at Bercy was very ill, and it was only on the Wednesday evening that I was able to go and inquire for her. I found myself in one of these houses which might well make up of themselves a whole village, and a very poor one it would be. I crossed a long and very populous court; then I climbed three stairs, very poor and dark; at the end of a passage I saw some persons talking, whom I asked if I could see Hélène André. A man, without speaking, made me come into a barely furnished room, where I saw a large bed, and laid on it the mortal remains of the child I came to visit. "There is Hélène André," said her father to me.

The sorrow of that father and mother was heart-rending, and, weeping together, we prayed to Him who had given and who had taken away. I heard that for a long time Hélène had spoken to her father and mother of the joy she should have in going to her first communion. She was fourteen years old, but not until to-day, in death, was she clothed with the white robe of communion. Madame H—— had gone to see her some days ago. "Oh," said the young invalid, "I am so glad she came; I never wished her to go away again!" But she suffered terribly; in her pain she twisted and bent a ring that she prized very much. The last three days she was delirious. But God permitted that shortly before her departure she was able to say "Adieu," or rather "Au revoir," to her friends. She kissed her father, then her mother and brother, and two dear friends. Her father came near her again for one more embrace. She pointed up to the sky, "as if to tell me," said her father, "that now she was going to the arms of a Father in heaven." She clasped her hands, and in that attitude she departed to join the great multitude who, with

palms and white robes, have gone before us into the eternal
country, and sing before the throne of God the songs of
praise, begun even here in sorrow and conflict.

F. CHRISTOL.

*Translated Extract from Letter of a Girl of Twelve to One
of the Paris Sabbath-school Teachers.*

It will interest our readers to notice how firmly this
child, trained in the Roman views of penance, has grasped
the free gift of God in the Gospel :—

"It was through you that I have learned to love our
Lord Jesus ; for before I thought I loved Him, but I did
not know the way. We thought, Mother and I, that in
order to gain heaven it was necessary to do penance, or to
make some great sacrifice ; indeed, we did not know how.
But these dear meetings have given us the light, and we are
no longer in darkness, as formerly. You have enlightened
us, as well as those other gentlemen whom we heard at the
large meetings, which we always attend with such pleasure,
where we learn the truth that it is not necessary to make
such efforts, but that it is by faith that we have eternal life
with our Lord Jesus ; only to observe His commandments
and believe that He has really died for the sins of each one
of us ; that we had merited death, but that our Saviour has
died in our place, and that by His death our sins are forgiven ; then also He gives us the gift of eternal life, that
is to say freely. It is enough to know that we are guilty.
Let us come to Him with all our sins, and, as these gentlemen
tell us, ' whosoever believeth in Him has eternal life.' It
is a gift. Mother, as well as I, loves our Saviour, and we
ask Him every day (for our Saviour is love) to come to our
help, for we have so much need of His support ; and when
my little sisters, who are now far away from us, are brought
back (we ask it with all our heart), we will make them know
the great love of the Lord for us. They are still in the

dark, more than we, for no one has instructed them, as has been done in your meetings. If one has the desire, one can understand enough to find the way of salvation, which we little thought was so simple ; for we desire with all our heart that all who hear may believe and be saved. We bless the day when we have known these meetings, which have made us know and love our Saviour, Jesus Christ.

"A. T."

A Paris Boy's Letter to his Teacher.

At a meeting of the Edinburgh collectors, Mr. Greig read the following letter he had received from one of the boys attending the Ménilmontant meeting :—

Translation.

" PARIS, *May 25th*, 1880.

" DEAR SIR,—Philip Lemoine told me on Sunday that you had gone to Scotland ; he gave me also your address, and so I am writing to you.

[After telling his teacher of the illness of one of the workers, and how the " Lord Jesus had preserved her " during it, he goes on to say,—]

" Do the children of Scotland love the Lord Jesus ? are there many among them who are converted ? I have learned also that an Association of Christian children has been formed in Scotland. Will you be so good as to tell me what this Association may be which the little Parisians are invited to join ?

" I beg you also to send me an English picture-card, as a souvenir of this letter. If I had any of these picture-cards, I should send you some to give to the Scotch children ; unfortunately, I have none.

" I should like to know if you are soon coming back to see us at the Ménilmontant meeting ; if you do not come back soon, I shall write to you often.

"I hope you will write to me when this letter reaches you ; please write me, that I may be sure that you have received this letter ; it is so far.

"My parents and myself hope that you are quite well.

"You won't, perhaps, remember my name, but you know me by sight.

"Expecting a reply, this is my address—

"GUSTAVE DECHAMBOUX,
"3, Rue des Poiriers,
"à Charonne,
"Paris, 20th Arrondissement, Seine.

"I finish my letter by warmly shaking your hand.

"P.S.—Write to me as soon as possible."

Clémence Delaunay, the Cripple Girl of Faubourg St. Antoine.

Miss Matheson has given us the following particulars about a little French girl :—

"Some time ago, in all the children's meetings in the Faubourg St. Antoine, and at the weekly Bible-class, were always to be seen two little friends sitting side by side : Clémence Delaunay, a little deformed girl, with a face that told of years of suffering ; and Félicie Danot, a pale fragile child.

"After a time Clémence became very ill. Some friends, who took great interest in her, repeatedly tried to induce her to go to the Hospital of the Deaconesses, where she would have skilful nursing and many comforts lacking in her poor home. But she begged to be allowed to remain with her parents. She lingered many months in constant suffering. Often when I visited her, I thought it must be the last time, and the poor little sufferer would soon be at rest. But several months passed before Jesus called her home. Her little friend spent every spare moment beside her bed, and related to her all that was said in the meetings. Often would they read the Bible and sing together. They knew that they must soon part, but with joy and confidence they gave each other *rendez-vous* in heaven with Jesus. Clémence was always sweet and patient ; never a murmur escaped her lips. It was thus she tried to follow Christ, and now we feel thankful that God kept His little one in her own home, to bear witness for Him. Her parents wondered at her peace and joy ; that she could sing in the long days of want and suffering was a mystery to them. Her father was given to drink, and her mother had a hard struggle to procure necessary comforts. She parted with one article of furniture after another. When the mother was wearied with the toil and struggle, Clémence would read some comforting words from the Bible to her.

"One night she passed in such agony that she could not lie still in any position ; but, while the contortions of her body showed her pain, her lips breathed nothing but prayer and submission to her Saviour Jesus. Another day, her mother, going upstairs to where she had left her child alone, heard a clear, steady voice singing,

> Oh, depth of mercy ! can it be,
> That gate was left ajar for me?

She could hardly believe it was her daughter, who had not sung for more than a year. The father, awestruck, left off his habits of drinking ; the mother, weeping, said she was willing to let her daughter depart on seeing the joy she had in Christ. Before she bid farewell to her parents, she made them promise always to go to the meetings at the mission-hall. Father and mother have faithfully kept that promise ; we have good hope that the father is breaking off his bad habits, and the mother's one desire is that Clémence's Saviour may be her Saviour, and that she may have a place

beside her little girl in glory.   The other day she said, 'We
know Clémence is in heaven with Jesus.'   Then alluding to
the idea so prevalent here, she added, 'She prays for us.'
I replied, 'You do not need Clémence to pray for you.
Jesus is our Advocate ; His pleading can never fail.   We
have only to put our cause into His hands, and He asks no
payment : all is free.'   She followed me to the door, then
said slowly, as if musing over what I had said, 'Then we
have only to trust altogether to Jesus ; there is nothing else.'

"We invited both parents to a Bible-class at the mission-
hall, adding, 'Clémence would like you to go.'   At once
they gladly promised to come.   The mother had been in
the habit of earning a good deal of money by selling fruit
and vegetables, but had been obliged to part with her barrow
during Clémence's illness.   When a friend brought her
some money to buy another barrow, she expressed her thanks,
and then added, 'But I will thank God.   He sent you.
Oh, He has never forsaken us ; He has supplied all our
wants wonderfully' (alluding to the help of kind friends
during the illness of their child).   It was then suggested
that she should show her desire to serve God by deciding
not to use the new barrow on His holy day.   It was no
slight proof to ask, as costermongers sell more on that day
than any other.   She rejoiced us by answering that she had
thought of this already, and did not mean to sell on Sunday."

Miss Matheson adds :—" I was visiting a great invalid in
the Faubourg St. Antoine, whose children frequent the
mission-hall.   When I spoke to her of a sure hope beyond the
grave, and the joy of going to be with Christ, she said she
did not see how we could have such confidence.   I had
scarcely time to reply before a little voice said, 'Celui qui
croit en moi vivra, quand même il serait mort.' *   It was the
voice of her own little son."

* "He that believeth on Me, though he were dead, yet shall he
live."

The Children's Hymns.

Extract from a letter of M. Savy, colleague of the Rev.
D. Robert, director of the Lille, Roubaix, and Croix branch
of the Mission :

"While passing, a fortnight ago, along one of the streets
of Roubaix, I suddenly overheard children's voices singing
with much energy a well-known hymn, which we had taught
our Sunday scholars a few months before. Wishing to
know a little more, and to find out who was the singer, I
went forward in the direction of the sound, and, to my
surprise, I perceived in a narrow street a group of little
girls all kneeling on chairs placed in a row ; they had
their hands folded, and the eldest of them was beating time
to the hymn whose music and words had attracted my
attention. The words which they were singing were
these :

> Je suis petit, mais peu importe,
>   Du bon Berger je suis l'agneau ;
> Je puis donc entrer par la porte
>   Qui mène au ciel tout Son troupeau, etc., etc.

"I cannot describe to you the pleasure I felt on seeing
the children in this attitude, singing with such perfect
seriousness. I at once passed on, so as not to disturb or
interrupt them ; for they knew me well, being all scholars
of the Rue des Fondeurs.

"Let me give you another fact, no less delightful than
the preceding, which shows clearly that the Divine seed
cast into these young hearts is not lost. A very intelligent
girl, who never fails to give most satisfactory answers to all
the questions put to her, on Sunday and Thursday, in our
meetings at Roubaix (for she is never absent from school),
and who sometimes repeats, almost word for word, the
stories read in the *Feuille du Dimanche,* or in the *Rayon de*

Soleil, or those which are told by the superintendent,—this child had brought me a bouquet of flowers, thinking to give me pleasure by so doing, an expectation which certainly did not prove false. After thanking her, I said that I should like to pay a visit to her parents, which she said would give her great pleasure. Accordingly I called on them. Two out of the three children who come to our meetings had preceded me ; the third wished to stay with me and show me the way. When I reached the house, they all took to jumping with glee, crying out, 'How delightful! how delightful ! M. Savy has come to see us !' When quiet was a little restored, the father said to me, ' I do not know, sir, what you do to our children, but since they have begun to go to your school I find them quite changed. They sing from morning to night beautiful hymns, which we are very fond of listening to ; and I assure you that, if we wished to keep them from going to school, it would be very difficult. Let me just give you an example,' added he. 'A week ago, the youngest had gone off to play ; when she returned, her two sisters had already left for school. She asked what o'clock it was, and, on being told, exclaimed, "Oh, dreadful ! I shall be late," and instantly was off like a flash, leaving her dinner untouched. And then, too,' continued the father, ' see how carefully they keep their *bons points,* their *Rayons de Soleil,* etc., etc. They have each a box, which they keep most carefully ; and we are very well pleased that they should, for these are very good little papers, and I never fail to read them with pleasure.'

"Who can calculate the good which these papers can do, by the blessing of God, in the numerous families where they enter ? Who can tell the immense good which can be done in the hearts of these dear little ones by the lessons from the Bible, the stories told them, and these beautiful Gospel hymns which we sing? God only knows."

Virgin Soil.

In one of our children's meetings the lesson for the day chanced to be on prayer and the gift of the Holy Spirit. The speaker, thinking that of the two evils, repeating words destitute of meaning and straining the intelligence to grasp ideas unsuited to their age, the latter was the less, proceeded to explain to the children what was meant by praying for spiritual graces, using language and illustrations so thoroughly level with their intellectual capacities, that the greatest quietness reigned in the *salle*, and intelligence seemed to beam on every face. The teacher, greatly encouraged, finished by saying, " Now, how many of you have already prayed for spiritual graces?" Up went several hands, but on investigation most of these morning devotions resolved themselves into repetitions, more or less exact, of the Lord's Prayer. One boy, however, the model boy of the school, persisted in his assertion that to the " Notre Père " he had added something which answered to his teacher's description of a prayer for spiritual graces. A little encouragement overcame his shyness, and he repeated word for word the petitions he had used, which a quick-witted *monitrice* got him to write down on the spot. Except for the separation into lines, I give it exactly as he wrote it, not only as a curiosity in phonetic spelling, but to show how very careful we require to be in inquiring whether our pupils attach to a word we use the same idea as we do. In all good conscience the child thought that this rigmarole was a prayer, and because it was something additional to the usual " Notre Père," it must be the additional requests for special grace of which his teacher spoke :—

La sin vierge s'enva par les champs,
Dans sont chemin rencontre Saint Jean.
" Saint Jean, où devenez-vous ? "
" Je vient de faire mon aves salue."

"Avez-vous vu
Mon enfant Jésus ? "
" Oui, ma trés chére damme,
Je l'ai vue
A l'arbre de la croix,
Qui avait les mains cloué,
Le côté percé,
Et la tête couronnée
D'épines blanches."

" Ceux qui diront matin et soir cette 'raison-là ne véront jamais les flâmes de l'enfer."*

The original can be found, correctly spelled, and with occasional slight modification, in many a Catholic book of devotion.

Do you still wonder, reader, that the authorities have forbidden the teaching of prayers (?) in the public schools by the monks and nuns?   C. E. GREIG.

---

* *Translation.*

" As the Holy Virgin was walking through the fields, on her way she met St. John.

" 'St. John, whence come you ? '

" 'I have just been saying my prayers.'

" 'Have you seen my Child Jesus ? '

" 'Yes, dear lady, I saw Him on the Cross, with nails in His hands, His side pierced, and on His head a crown of white thorns.'

" Those who repeat this prayer morning and night will never see the flames of hell."

EXTERIOR OF THE SALLE, BOULEVARD DE SÉBASTOPOL.

CONCLUSION.

BY PASTOR THEODORE MONOD.

DEAR MR. McALL,—You request me to write the concluding chapter of a book which you give me no opportunity to read. While appreciating your friendly confidence, I feel sadly embarrassed before the unusual task of having to draw a conclusion from premises unknown. I am bound, however, not to disappoint you, and if it should prove, after all, that my conclusion fits in with the premises at which I can merely guess, the fact of itself will strikingly demonstrate the substantial agreement and perfect harmony that exist among all those who have the privilege of being in any way connected with your Mission.

These, then, are my conclusions :—

1. A missionary work among the working classes of France has been carried on for fifteen years, on new lines.

2. The work originated, as all good things do, in a small but living seed, the planting of the heavenly Father's hand (Matt. xv. 13).

3. It has proved itself well adapted to the national character, as well as to the spiritual need, of the French people.

4. It has prospered, under the blessing of God, and s steadily, increasingly, effectually spreading the light and the saving power of the Gospel.

5. It has the sympathy of all the evangelical Churches in the land, and the hearty co-operation of many of their pastors and members.

6. It thus exerts a quickening influence upon the Churches themselves, as well as upon the people at large, and tends to promote Christian fellowship, through united labour.

7. It is ever ready for any improvement in its methods that may tend to increase its efficiency in view of the spiritual welfare of the people.

8. While meeting a need that is not met by the regular Church organisations (from which the bulk of our people keep aloof), it results eventually in the accession of new members to the various Churches, a process quietly and constantly going on.

9. If France (not to say the Continent) is to escape from the fearful calamity anticipated by many a thoughtful observer (Dr. Wylie, for instance)—namely, from being ground to powder " between the upper and nether millstones of Romanism and Atheism "—such agencies as the McAll Mission are among the most effectual means of so influencing the public mind as to avert the wrath of God and the fury of men.

10. It cannot be too clearly understood by our friends abroad (chiefly, of course, in Great Britain and America) that this enterprise is, emphatically, *a* MISSION, although it be carried on in a civilised country, and alongside of other evangelical work. It has been originated for France by Christians who do not themselves belong to France. French Protestants did not call for it, did not organise it, hardly understood it at first ; they were slow to welcome it or to lend it a helping hand ; and even now they contribute but

meagerly, as a body, towards its support. Whether they are to be blamed for it or not ; whether they may be expected to contribute more largely ; whether one should entertain the hope of seeing, at some future period, the work carried on chiefly by "the natives" themselves, are questions altogether foreign to our "order of the day." The "McAll *Mission*" is, at present, *a* MISSION, and, as such, must be carried on by those who have taken the initiative, and to whom belong both the merit and the responsibility of this new, this excellent, this blessed agency for the evangelisation of France. It is, therefore, no more than right that the Protestants of more favoured lands should organise for the support of this Mission.

11. Let any one reflect upon the influence exerted throughout the world by the example and literature of France, and consider the importance of purifying such influence. It is no exaggeration to say that our Christian friends in England and America, while they are doing good to us, will be working also for the benefit of their own country.

12. *Twelve* is the perfect number, and with it I come to my summing up, which is this :—

The "Mission Populaire" founded by Mr. McAll fully deserves the generous, persevering, prayerful support of all who sincerely say, "Thy kingdom come !"

That every reader of this book may become a helper in this work is the earnest hope of

Yours most respectfully and affectionately,

THEODORE MONOD.

PARIS, *Nov. 22nd,* 1886.

COMMITTEE OF DIRECTION OF THE McALL MISSION.

Honorary President:
Rev. R. W. McALL, 28, Villa Molitor, Auteuil, Paris.

Directors:

Rev. C. E. Greig, M.A.	Eugène Réveilland.
Rev. Dr. Hough.	Ruben Saillens.
Rev. W. W. Newell, Jun.	Louis Sautter.
Emile Rouilly.	

Treasurer: Léon Rieder.

Finance Secretary: William Soltau.

MISSIONARIES IN PARIS.

Rev. S. R. Brown.	Aided by MM. les Pasteurs
Rev. S. H. Anderson.	Theodore Monod and T.
Etienne Sagnol.	Lorriaux, M. Guillaume
Alexander Donaldson.	Van der Beken, and many
M. le Pasteur Cerisier.	other pastors and friends.

Superintendent of Juvenile Mission:
Rev. C. E. Greig, M.A., 40, Boulevard de Reuilly, Paris.

Medical Superintendent of Dispensaries:
Dr. D. Elie Anderson, 21, Avenue de la Grande Armée, Paris.

Consulting Physician:
Dr. H. Richardson Darcus, 7, Rue Poisson, Paris.

Honorary Director and Representative in England:
F. Dundas Chauntrell, Les Ombrages, Sion Hill, Bath.

Offices of the Mission: 28, Villa Molitor, Auteuil, Paris.

The following Treasurers of Auxiliaries, etc., will be glad to receive contributions for the McAll Mission :—

ENGLAND.

London : Frank A. Bevan, 54, Lombard Street, E.C.; Lady Congleton, 53, Great Cumberland Place, W.; Messrs. Morgan and Scott, 12, Paternoster Buildings, E.C.; Rev. H. Noel, M.A., Woking Station, Surrey; Rev. R. S. Ashton, B.A., 11, Blomfield Street, E.C.

Liverpool : William Crosfield, J.P., 8, Temple Court; James Cullen, 13, Rumford Street.

Leeds : Fred. R. Spark, Hyde Terrace.

Bristol : Samuel D. Wills, J.P., Castle Green.

Bath : F. Dundas Chauntrell, Sion Hill.

Plymouth : R. Reynolds Fox, Westbrook.

Sheffield : J. H. Barber, J.P., Sheffield Banking Company.

SCOTLAND.

Edinburgh : John Brewis, C.A., 5, North St. David Street.

Glasgow : Robert Pirrie, 207, West George Street; W. M. Wiseley, 27, St. Vincent Place.

Dundee : J. Dickson Dodds, 2, India Buildings.

Aberdeen : John Edmond, 10, Bridge Street.

Perth : James Coates.

UNITED STATES.
American McAll Association.
President : Mrs. Mariné J. Chase.
Treasurer : Miss Frances Lea.
Foreign Secretary : Mrs. J. M. Longacre.
Offices : 1622, Locust Street, Philadelphia.

LIST OF STATIONS.

PARIS.

La Concorde,* 23, Rue Royale (near La Madeleine) ; Hôtel de Ville,† 10, Boulevard de Sébastopol ; Boulevards, ‡ 8, Boulevard Bonne Nouvelle ; Montmartre, No. 1, 56, Boulevard Barbès (formerly Ornano) ; Faubourg St. Antoine, 142, Rue du Faubourg St. Antoine ; Batignolles, 3, Rue des Dames ; Les Ternes, 59, Avenue de Wagram ; Quartier Latin, 62, Rue Monge ; La Villette, No. 1, 90, Rue d'Allemagne ; Popincourt, No. 1, 123, Boulevard Voltaire ; Ménilmontant, 39, Rue de Ménilmontant ; Belleville (School), 112, Rue de Belleville ; Grenelle, 59, Rue Letellier ; Passy, 62, Rue Boissière ; Bercy, 76, Boulevard de Bercy ; Montparnasse, 74, Rue des Fourneaux ; Gare d'Ivry, 12, Rue Nationale ; Gros Caillou, 100, Rue St. Dominique ; Vaugirard, 373, Rue de Vaugirard ; Petit Montrouge, 79, Rue Daguerre ; La Villette, No. 2, 121, Rue de Meaux ; Quartier du Temple, 77, Rue Charlot ; Popincourt, No. 2, 153, Avenue Ledru Rollin ; Montmartre, No. 2, 2 bis, Rue Berthe.

ENVIRONS OF PARIS.

Versailles, 81, Rue de la Paroisse ; Puteaux, 8, Rue Godefroy ; Montreuil-sous-Bois, 218 bis, Rue de Paris ; Pantin, 33, Rue de Magenta ; Boulogne-sur-Seine, 2, Rue Mollien ; Ivry (ville), 66, Rue du Liégat ; Nanterre, 12,

---

* Evangelistic meeting every week-evening at 8.15, and on Sundays at 4.30.

† Evangelistic meeting every evening at 8, and on Sundays at 3 p.m. and 8 p.m.

‡ Evangelistic meeting every evening, Sunday included, at 8.15.

Rue du Chemin de Fer; Sainte Gemme, and other villages ; Melun, Chapelle Evangélique ; Creil, Route de Montataire.

MARSEILLES.

59, Boulevard National; 43, Boulevard Baille; 67, Chemin d'Endoume ; 38, Rue de la République ; 2, Rue des Minimes ; 2, Boulevard Romieu.

NICE.

Boulevard de la Gare ; 2, Rue de la Préfecture ; Villefranche-sur-Mer, Salle du Théâtre ; Cagne, Café de la Villette.

CANNES.

6, Rue des Marchés.

MENTONE.

Villa les Grottes.

CORSICA.

Ajaccio.

LYONS.

Les Brotteaux, 89, Avenue de Saxe; La Guillotière, Grande Rue de la Guillotière ; La Croix Rousse, 1, Rue du Mail.

BORDEAUX.

Les Chartrons, 6, Cours St. Louis ; St. Nicholas, 15, Rue de Beaufleury ; Meriadec, 55, Rue de Belfort ; La Bastide, 14, Rue Durand ; Chartreuse, 53, Rue de Vincennes; 99, Rue de Naujac.

BOULOGNE-SUR-MER.

Central Station, Rue Adolphe Thiers ; Marine Quarter, 12, Rue du Parc.

LA ROCHELLE AND ROCHEFORT.

La Rochelle, 6, Rue du Temple ; Rochefort, 30, Rue du Champ de Foire.

LILLE, ROUBAIX, CROIX, AND DUNKIRK.

Roubaix, Rue des Fondeurs ; Croix, Salle de Musique ;
Lille, Fives ; Dunkirk, Rue du Jeu de Paume.

ST. ETIENNE.

7, Rue de la Banque ; 23, Rue St. Honoré ; 28, Rue St.
Jacques ; Firming.

SAINTES AND COGNAC.

Saintes, Avenue Gambetta ; Cognac, Rue du Jardin
Public.

TOULOUSE.

105, Grand Rue du Faubourg St. Michel ; 46, Rue de la
Colombette ; 18, Rue des Trois Piliers.

MONTAUBAN.

Rue Lacapelle.

MONTPELLIER, CETTE, AND BEZIERS.

Montpellier, 39, Cours Gambetta ; Cette, 3, Rue l'Issanka ;
Beziers, 32, Rue de la Gare.

NANTES AND ST. NAZAIRE.

Nantes, 41, Grande Biesse ; St. Nazaire, 9, Rue de
l'Artillerie.

ALGIERS.

3, Rue Tanger.

---

*Clermont Ferrand, Auxerre, Alençon, Lorient, Brest, Rennes,
Clamecy, Tulle, Sotteville, Perpignan, Magny-en-Vexin,
Lourches, Fontenay-le-Comte, Tunis, Calais.*

SUMMARY OF THE YEAR'S WORK, 1885.

Most of the figures have been taken in detail; the others are approximate.

PARIS.

French meetings for adults	3,961
Aggregate attendance at ditto	405,640
French after-meetings and prayer-meetings (291), attendance	18,346
Adult Bible-classes and *Sociétés Fraternelles* (484), attendance	22,710
Ouvroirs (sewing meetings for poor women) (350), attendance	9,713
Aggregate attendance at adult religious meetings in Paris	456,159
Number of Sunday-school teachers . . .	209
Meetings held in Sunday-schools, and children's services	1,952
Attendance at ditto, Sundays	49,297
Ditto, week-days	68,769
Young women's meetings, Bible Union meetings, etc. (232), attendance	2,915
Aggregate juvenile attendance	120,981
Total of religious meetings in Paris . . .	7,270
Attendance at ditto	577,140

Increase of attendance for the year, 61,558.

Domiciliary visits	8,000
Bibles and Testaments issued	1,492
Books issued from lending libraries . .	5,000
Scripture portions distributed	8,896
Tracts, copies of *L'Ami de la Maison*, etc., distributed	221,491

The above numbers are exclusive of psalmody meetings.

Madame Dalencourt's meetings, Young Men's Christian Association meetings, and others for which the mission rooms are lent gratuitously. Weekly prayer-meeting of the mission workers, at 23, Rue Royale, Friday, 5 p.m.

GENERAL TOTALS FOR THE YEAR 1885.

PARIS AND THE PROVINCES.

Religious meetings for adults (12,357), attendance 799,610
Sunday-schools, children's services, young women's
    classes, etc. (3,681), attendance .   .   . 187,444
Total of religious meetings .   .   . 16,038
Total attendance at ditto 987,054
Increase for the year 84,933
Domiciliary visits 18,393
Bibles, Testaments, portions, tracts, and illus-
    trated papers circulated .   .   . 399,666

Printed by Hazell, Watson, & Viney, Ld., London and Aylesbury.